For Whom the Wedding Bells Toll

Joshua Lee

Published by Joshua Lee, 2021.

FOR WHOM THE WEDDING BELLS TOLL

First edition. March 12, 2021.

Copyright © 2021 Joshua Lee.

ISBN: 979-8215781067

Written by Joshua Lee.

To Christopher, Julie, and Natalie for giving me the inspiration to make this book a reality.

Prologue

NEWS FLASH! SUPERMODEL Cherrie Lopez-Harrison, newly wed to NBA superstar Harry Madison, had then attempted to get married to Navy SEAL platoon commander Theodore Lincoln. Almost overnight, the press had swiftly seized coverage of the unfolding drama, sure to go down as the celebrity scandal of the year.

Magazines and newspapers floated headlines, attacking Lincoln as a "bridal thief," blaming him for pursuing, seducing, and stealing away Cherrie, regarded by the press as the Eighth Wonder for her beauty. Others had charged her for deceptively covering up her former marriage, some wondered if she had been unable to file for divorce and had simply gone and attempted to marry another man.

That she had been married to Madison in the first place, it was news. They had been seen together in public and rumours of their being in a relationship had surfaced, but they never confirmed anything. It was therefore evident they had eloped, but several tabloids had written off their marriage as a publicity stunt.

The morning of the trial came with anticipation and anxiety riding high as the courtroom filled to capacity. Reporters in the stands were anxiously scribbling down notes and making sketches and phones were ringing constantly. Even as they spoke, news articles were already aired online with the breaking news. Each outlet gave their spin on the whole story, eager to read into the unexpected affair.

The judge, an overweight man in his fifties, briskly entered the courtroom with an air of authority and business. Immediately, the bailiff called for everyone to rise, as the judge climbed up to his bench.

"Be seated," the judge requested, and then the courtroom fell silent, like the calm before the storm. The cases were about to be presented. High-profile stories having taken place outside the public eye were about to be released.

For a moment, the judge sat quietly, scanning the courtroom, taking in the whole scene, from the reporters to the public. He felt the anticipation and he himself was interested in bringing forth the truth about the case. Finally, he asked his bailiff to read out the charges.

"The people vs. Madison, charges of marital bigamy," the bailiff read out. "Representing prosecution is state attorney Manuel J. Monroe. Representing Madison is Counsellor Malcolm R. Bush."

"Thank you," the judge said. "Will the prosecution present their case?"

"Thank you, your honour," the prosecutor declared. "Of the different crimes we have prosecuted in the State of Michigan, this is the first case of attempted bigamy. Why this would happen, we do not know, but we have documented evidence that Mrs. Cheryl Madison has been recognized by the state as legally wed to Mr. Henry Madison, and has been caught in her attempt to illegally marry Mr. Theodore Lincoln, two weeks prior to this date."

"Thank you," the judge continued as the prosecutor sat. "Will the defence give their testimony?"

"Your honour," the defending lawyer stated, "Mrs. Madison recognizes her error, and wishes to have her marriage annulled. It was never consummated, and she shall be free to marry whomever she chooses."

A murmur arose within the crowd. Annulment was rarely filed, and often difficult to prove. The defence would have their work cut out for them.

"Will the prosecution call forth their witness?" the judge requested.

"We call on Mr. Henry Madison," Monroe announced.

"Mr. Madison to the stand," the bailiff called out. A murmur arose in the crowd as the star player for the Miami Heat strode toward the stand, carrying himself with his usual swagger of confidence.

Harry, also known by his nickname, Molokai Express, was a fast-rising star in his mid-twenties. Widely considered to be the next Kobe Bryant, he had been drafted first overall by the Los Angeles Clippers, and during his seven years with the franchise, he would lead them out of the league basement – to two consecutive league championships. In the process, he helped earn the Clippers a nation-wide following, as basketball fans coast to coast eagerly tuned in to see this new wunderkind.

The honeymoon however would not last. Upon hitting free agency, in a move reminiscent of LeBron James leaving the Cavaliers, he would sign an offer sheet with the Miami Heat. Fans were outraged at his defection, for he seemed to be destined to remain a Clipper for life. It was apparent to many that he had merely switched teams just to create a controversy. And while in Florida, he had met Cherrie Lopez-Harrison, supermodel, reigning Miss Universe, and cheerleader with the Heat.

Harry was an impressive looking guy. He had a lean, six foot three inch frame. He had a prominent dimple on his chin. He had blazing blue eyes. His blonde hair had a crew cut.

"Do you swear to tell the truth, the whole truth, and nothing but the truth?" the bailiff asked.

"I do," Harry responded.

"Mr. Madison," Monroe requested, "please tell the court about your involvement with the defendant and your marriage to her."

The courtroom, growing silent seemed to lean forward as one as the superstar proceeded to tell his story.

Harry's Story: Chapter 1

TO EVERYONE, THERE'S a different meaning to what life is about. For me, it is carpe diem, seize the day. Get all that you can, strive for the next level. And when opportunities knock, seize on it. Take whatever comes your way. Don't wait for tomorrow and don't let anything stand in your way. That's how I roll in all I do.

I inherited a love of basketball early in life. As a three-year-old, I had been shooting hoops in a toy net in our backyard. As I grew older, I began to get more serious, enrolling in junior basketball camps and tournaments, along with my older brother Fred. It was our dream to play professional basketball, but between the two of us, only I received the call.

I was driven to be the best player I could be, and I worked hard between practice and homework, practicing with the ball. Fred and I would often square off for matches to 21 in our elementary school gym, and being three years older, he always won until I was nine.

By that time, I had been the best player in my age group for both basketball camps and the elementary school team. I was winning several awards and scholarships, and by now had enough money in scholarships to get through college.

I had managed to set the bar high, but my father, who coached the high school basketball team, set the bar even higher. "You know, Harry," he had said, after I had won my second match. "You are ready for a whole new level. How would you like to play against some of the boys from high school with your brother?"

For a moment, I saw Fred cringe. It was indeed a tough challenge, going up against bigger, more seasoned players. But I lived for the challenge, and readily agreed to it. We agreed to set our match for the following week.

All week long, Fred dragged me out to the park, begging me to show him all the tricks I've learned. Every evening, he would read through basketball books I had borrowed from the library, picking up on every trick, which we would then practice together the following afternoon. By the end of the week, he managed to pick up more skills.

"You know, Harry," he had said after one practice, "I think you're simply a basketball prodigy. You're picking up on skills much quicker than I did at your age. You could be the next Kobe Bryant."

I thought about his words for a moment. "Well," I said, "the first test comes tomorrow against the bullies." I suddenly passed the ball behind him, but before he could reach back to get it, I whirled past him, and shot it into the net. "Yes, we can beat them."

Fred could only look on in disbelief.

The day of the match, after school, we invited some of our friends over to come see the match. We came to the court to see the high school team practicing in full swing. We sat down by the sidelines and waited.

"So you're seriously going to take on those boys?" Jack, one of my friends, asked.

"That's the deal," Fred said. "That's our reward for Harry beating me in last week's match."

"That's crazy," said Joe, another of our friends. "You may be the best player in school, but com'on, who can stand up to these guys. They're really going to kick your butts."

Just then, a group of cheerleaders strode into the room and sat down right behind us.

"So when is the big match?" I heard one of them ask. "Coach Madison says there's a big match with Rob and Greg against two out-of-school stars this afternoon."

"That would be us," I said, turning around.

"Are you kidding?" another girl asked, cracking up. The girls began giggling with her. "Is coach seriously–"

"Hey," Fred cut her off, "we're his sons. We know more about basketball, because we were born playing basketball. You'll just wait and see."

Dad's whistle soon cut me off. "All right boys," he announced, "we've got the grand elementary-high school showdown this afternoon. Hailing from your local Cedar Valley High are Robert and Gregory Garfield. And representing Cedar Valley Elementary are Fred and Harry Madison."

As the two older took to the court, Dad added, "We've got the cheerleading squad watching you. You don't want to be humiliated before two kids, do you?"

"Don't worry coach," Rob said to him. "Taking on two harmless kids should be no challenge."

He then went over the rules. It was to be a ten-minute regulation match between the two teams, each of whom were allowed one timeout. With that, we faced off. As Dad threw the ball into the air, Fred somehow caught the ball and tipped it over to me. I immediately whirled toward the net, twisting around Greg, before netting a jump shot.

Just then, I saw a few more of the older kids walk into the gym. They must have heard about how two elementary age boys were challenging two of their own basketball heroes to a match. They looked stunned to see this little kid suddenly net a jump shot.

Rob, taking the ball, checked it in to me. As I passed it to him, he immediately tossed the ball over to Greg, who proceeded to dunk the ball. Game was tied 2-2.

"We'll never be able to dunk," Fred complained. "What can we do?"

"Use your head," I told him.

The game wore on. Greg and Rob took an early lead by firing a series of jump shots and dunks that neither Fred nor I could defend.

After only four minutes, they had an 18-5 lead, when Fred called a timeout.

"Okay," he said to me. "We're down 18-5. These boys are really taking us seriously, and there's no way we can stop one of their jump shots or dunks."

"Defend down low," I said. "We have to stay on each of those boys and defend by making steals. Whenever we get the ball, pass it to me, and get into scoring position. I'll pass and you shoot, or I'll take a shot myself."

We resumed our game. I took the ball and quickly eluded Rob. Spotting Fred deke around Greg, I snapped him a pass. He dribbled out to the three-point zone, and netted a shot.

On the next play, I followed through on a fade away three-pointer shot of my own, following a quick steal from a dribbling Greg.

Suddenly, Fred and I had found our momentum. I'd somehow managed to anticipate Greg's and Rob's moves, and by sticking with them, Fred and I managed to slow them down and find ways to keep them from making the jump shots and dunks that we dreaded. Whenever we had the ball, we knew how they were going to defend us, and with a quick pass or a snappy spin, Fred and I would get through them and put the ball in the net.

The crowd on the sidelines were watching in amazement. Not expecting much of a contest for Fred and me, I heard some of them begin cheering for us, while jeering Greg and Rob. Shouts of "Here comes MJ in the making!" or "Greggy and Robby are beaten by babies!" could be heard. As Fred and I gained momentum, Rob and Greg were getting frustrated and humiliated, desperate not to be made fools of.

With seconds left on the clock, Fred snapped me the ball. I spun away from Greg and snapped one more shot to take the lead. On the ensuing checking-in of the ball, Rob grabbed the ball and drove hard for the net. I stood right in his path, as Fred stayed with him. Rob made for a layup, knocking me down on my back to net the shot, just as time expired.

My father disqualified the shot. "That's a charge! Fred and Harry win," he announced.

By now, nearly half the school had gathered in the gymnasium. They got up and cheered, amazed that two elementary-age boys took on two high school players.

I got up as Rob came over to me. "Bold move," he said. "I hope you weren't hurt."

"No," I said. "I deliberately sacrificed my body to win."

"You boys were unbelievable," Greg added, coming up beside him. "You should keep up this game. It'll be a great chance to fetch some girls."

"Back off," Fred said. "We're not in for the girls."

"Oh, wait and see," Greg retorted with a chuckle. "They love guys who can be real heroes, in the NBA."

For the next twenty minutes, people kept congratulating Fred and me. Some people even asked for our autographs. But when it was all over, it was time for a grand banana split, a treat fit for victory.

Greg was right about one thing. Basketball could be an effective ticket to fetching girls. I began to realize that after entering high school, when I attended the junior high school dance with a girl from the cheerleading squad.

I was an awkward dancer that first date, and a couple of times, we moved too quickly and fell to the floor. Embarrassed, I merely laughed and remarked, "Oops, this isn't basketball," as we picked ourselves up and carried on.

Inside, I was worried about making a fool of myself, the first time I was ever concerned about it. A year ago, I couldn't care less about girls, but something was different this time. I looked into her eyes, and she seemed to be enjoying herself.

I lost my balance and we fell again, but she only laughed. "Dude, you ought to take dancing lessons," she said. By now, I could see a few other couples looking on us, and now I was really concerned I was making a fool of myself.

My worries went away that next day in school when I overheard that girl talking to her friends about having her date. She seemed not to care that I was such a clumsy dancer, rather she was laughing away as she talked about our date. Feeling comfortable, I made my way over to her.

"Well, if it isn't the Molokai Express," she began. "We were just talking about you."

This new name caught my curiosity. "Molokai Express?" I asked. "What's that?"

"It's an ocean current running through the islands of Hawaii," she replied. "It is so powerful, that you can't swim through it, lest you get swept away to Alaska."

"Oh, I get it," I replied with a grin. "You loved it when I swept you off your feet last night."

She laughed, and some of her friends managed a giggle as well. "And then you do that to the ball, every time you take to the court."

I grinned. Well, I saved myself the initial embarrassment and it looks like the girls would take to me after all.

And so I had a new nickname. Molokai Express, the guy who can sweep through the court and wash away the opposition. This nickname would stick with me throughout high school, and into my professional career. All from a passing remark from this one pretty girl from the cheerleading squad.

Chapter 2

I HAD A SURPRISE THE next year, my sophomore year in high school. My dad, still coaching the varsity high school team, had negotiated to move me to the varsity team, even though I was a year underage. Naturally, I welcomed the challenge.

This move generated much attention, especially from some jealous parents. They believed that he was simply playing favourites. But before long, I began to show them why I was moved. We had a strong season that year, going undefeated for our first four games, and I would lead the way in scoring. By the following spring, we were reckoned a strong force, not only within the district, but we were even considered a contender for the state championship.

I can still remember that game, playing for the district championships in our building. There was a buzz in the air, as the gymnasium was packed to capacity, for it was our first ever appearance in the finals. The cheerleaders continued to do their dances in our school colours.

We did our team huddle, and my brother, who served as captain did the talking. "We had come this far," he had said. "Let's play together. We can win this game." With that, we turned and took to the court.

On that first toss-up, we lost the ball to the other team. Their opposing center had passed the ball off to his power forward and they began to move in toward our zone. But somehow, I knew what he was going to do, and called for my brother Fred, playing small forward, to cut in front of him.

Predictably, the guy made a back pass, and I saw their point guard moving in to receive. I quickly spun and snatched the ball, driving hard down the lane. Their centerman caught up and got in front of me, but I quickly spun, side-stepped him, and quickly scored a three-pointer shot.

The rest of the game unfolded. The opposition continued to bear down upon me, but when I was blocked, I could somehow find ways to get past them or to find an open teammate. More often than not, they could not stop me without drawing a foul, and I would then score on the free-throw. In the end, we would win the game with a score of 88-79.

I remembered in the final minute of play, when we were holding out a narrow lead. My centerman had managed to narrowly block a shot, before hitting me with a pass. I quickly surged down the lane, with the opponents in hot pursuit. They knew they had to stop me, but I was going to beat them one way or another. I drew a foul on an attempted fade away shot, and proceeded to inflict damage on the free throw.

Their coach called a timeout, and everyone moved over to the sidelines. Dad just told us to keep calm.

"We are in the lead now," he was saying. "Everyone just try and slow this game down, and keep them from scoring. We can do this."

We took to the court again, with seconds left on the clock. The opponents came out at us, firing their shots, but we stood our ground, counting out the seconds remaining. I remembered stealing the ball and moving a little slowly up the court, for I was out of breath. Their shooting guard stole the ball, but I quickly stayed with him as he fired a shot desperately as time expired.

I remembered everyone storming the court. Fireworks resounded and floating balloons were released. I had been mobbed by several others. It was total pandemonium.

Before long, the celebration settled down, and the team took its place in the center court, joined by the principal and a few other teachers. We were publically congratulated by the mayor of our town and several other officials. Eventually, they brought out the trophy and presented that to us. We posed for an official picture with it, and then it was passed about, so every player could have a chance to handle it.

The season was not over yet, for we were invited to participate in the California State tournament, which was held upstate in Sacramento. I remember we were all riding high with excitement as we took that bus trip up the bay toward the state capital. We were on our way to prove our mettle, and everyone looked to me to lead the charge.

Sadly, that charge ended, as we lasted only one game in that match. Our opponents knew they had to guard me. They pounced all over us that game, and we had no answer for them.

I was frustrated, but considering that it was the first trip to the finals for our school, it was still a breakthrough. On a personal level, I began to realize my potential as a player and was determined to live up to it.

Fred graduated that year and went on to enroll in UCLA law school. During the graduation ceremonies, I promised him that I would get us back to the state tournaments and win it for him.

The following year, I made good on the promise, practicing with the other guys. We pushed each other to go further than before all year. We would come up short this year in the district championships, but we still received the invite to the state tournaments, which we won outright.

From that point on, my basketball career really took flight. I enrolled in the Amateur American Union, where I had the opportunity to compete nationally, ultimately winning a national title in my senior year. Along the way, I met with many NBA stars and coaches and even received calls for corporate sponsorship.

After graduation, I would enroll at UCLA where Fred had been studying law while playing basketball for the UCLA Bruins. The team had made the Final Four every year he was there, but fell short of winning the national title. I would prove to be the missing piece to deliver them a national title.

Shortly after my freshman year in UCLA, I had entered the NBA draft, which had been held downtown at the Staples Center. I was widely regarded as the consensus number one pick by most scouts and commentators.

The Los Angeles Clippers, having finished last in league standings that year, held the first overall pick. I was disappointed, for I had grown up as a Lakers fan. It would be quite awkward to play for the forgotten cross-town rivals and be their long-awaited saviour.

As the draft begun, I tried to warm myself up to the idea of playing for the Clippers, a team that constantly drafted high, but could never break the ice. I had spoken with numerous reporters and pundits about the question at hand, could I be the one to lift them out of the cellar?

As the Clippers management team took to the stage, their general manager came up to the microphone.

"The Los Angeles Clippers are pleased to use our first pick to draft from the University of California, Los Angeles, shooting guard Harry Madison," he announced. Applause swept the room as I got up and made my way down to the stage, greeting the league commissioner, Gerald Washington, who ushered me onto the stage. I proceeded to shake hands with the Clippers management, who then gave me their jersey.

Unsure if I wanted to play for the Clippers, I held out two more years, during which I remained at UCLA, leading the Bruins to two more national titles, all the while speculation pervaded on when I would become professional. During that period, I received an invite to the national Olympic team, the only invitee not yet playing in the NBA. Coming off the bench behind the established NBA players, I'd nonetheless played a key role in leading the States to the gold medal.

After my third year at UCLA, I signed a contract with the Clippers, with Fred serving as my agent. The wait was over, for Harry Madison had finally arrived in the NBA.

Our first game came against the hometown Lakers, my childhood favourites, and a team still performing strongly. They were the defending champions from last year and were still in position to contend. Our team was green with young, inexperienced players.

The match drew much attention and the stands were filled to capacity. People had come to see the much-hyped rookies battle the defending champions, and I was eager to bring my game on.

It was a special feeling, walking into the arena and seeing the flashing lights shining down toward me. And just across the court from us stood the great legendary warriors led by centerman Neil McKinley and point guard Brian Nixon, my childhood heroes. And now, I was playing them.

On that first tossup, I managed to swoop in and steal the ball from Nixon and move across the court. But I was so overwhelmed with the thrill at that point, I could not focus for those first few minutes. I attempted a shot only for McKinley to block it and pass the ball up the court to Nixon, who in turn fed him with an ally-oop.

After the first five minutes of play, I was substituted off. I took a swig of water and tried to calm my nerves, as the battle raged on.

We continued to play tentatively even as the Lakers built up their lead. By the end of the second quarter, they were up 60-25. I had a few more shifts, but I was having difficulty adjusting to the professional league.

I knew that people were watching me, and I was determined to show them my mettle, lest I risk being a bust. Leading into the third quarter, during the team huddle, I gave my teammates a few words.

"We are here now," I said. "Let's go rise to the challenge and show them."

As we took to the court, I could hear a few people jeering us. I was determined to make them eat their words.

This time, I caught the ball and drove quickly for their net, deking past McKinley and scoring. That would be the start of the rally as we began to wake up. The Lakers, meanwhile, seemed slow to adjust, thinking we scored a few fluke points. But though others did not see it, we were gaining morale, determined to challenge the big boys. We had a strong third quarter, closing the score to 75-60.

It was only then when the Lakers awoke again. But we were determined to take them on. The fourth quarter was a fierce battle, with both teams rallying back and forth. But as the Lakers pushed and surged, we held strong and stayed with them. In the dying seconds, I recalled McKinley dunking a shot. They were up by three points, and we had less than ten seconds left. I seized the ball and made a cross-court toss, putting the ball in the net just as time expired.

The battle was going into overtime as we continued to fight. But as tired as my teammates were, we were energized to realize how we had come back against the mighty neighbours. The Lakers, on the other hand, were for the first time looking aghast at the newly competitive Clippers they were facing.

Indeed, we would bring things up in the tie-breaker frame. The Lakers hung on for a while, but it was evident they were running out of gas. Following a timeout, they did manage to keep up, and briefly take a two-point lead as the seconds wore down. I took the ball, sailed up the court and once again fired a shot from just within half a court to score the game-winning shot as time expired.

Pandemonium swept the place, for it was clear the Clippers had now arrived, and were for real. Indeed, we would show them our mettle, as we performed strongly that season, making the playoffs for the first time in several years. We were eliminated in the first round, but it was nonetheless the initial breakthrough.

At the end of the season, I was recognized as Rookie of the Year. I remembered coming onstage to receive the prize, beaming widely, knowing that I had indeed made it.

Despite the breakthrough, there were still many skeptics who doubted the team, which had been a perpetual bane of failure, only taking up wasted space in Los Angeles. Even Harry Madison could never turn the team around, or so a number of pundits claimed.

I remember the start of the following season, when team owner Tom Adams had granted a press conference. People were asking him what he expected this season, and one person even asked when I would be traded and whom he'd hope to receive in return. He brushed off those thoughts with one bold statement: "Mark my words, the Clippers will win the Larry O'Brien."

That offseason, the team had made several major free agent signings and trades, adding a few veteran players. The new-look Clippers were a good blend of experienced veterans and talented young players, all poised to make good on Adams' declaration.

It took us three seasons before we finally won the championship, facing off against the Lakers in the conference finals in a matchup that drew a national following. Defeating them in six games, we then faced off against the defending champion Boston Celtics, ultimately dethroning them in five.

It was the stuff of legend. There were moribund teams who had their share of superstars unable to lead them to winning and instead wanted out of town for greener pastures. No one ever could have expected the Clippers to suddenly win the championship after generations of futility. But after this magical season, we soon drew a following that would soon outpace the longstanding Lakers.

Chapter 3

CHERRIE CAME INTO MY life the following season, during a game against the Miami Heat, where she began serving as a cheerleader that year. I can clearly remember seeing her, during the pre-game dance. As the lights dimmed the intro video played on the screens overhead, and then suddenly the flame throwers fired off and the cheerleaders took to the court, waving their pom-poms. Spotlights shone down upon them, and I suddenly saw her, standing front and center with the girls.

I had known about this girl for a long time. A rising star in the modelling world, also known as the Eighth Wonder, she had been winning beauty pageants on nearly every level. She had appeared in numerous magazine covers and her posters had been selling rapidly. She had even appeared in a movie just the year before, and she wasn't a bad actress like most other "wanna-be actresses," even in the celebrity world.

To call her a beauty is a total understatement. Cherrie was like a gleaming golden sculpture, but a live one. She was five feet seven and very slender, but not too willowy. Her skin was perfectly tanned, delicate, but well-toned. She had shiny light bronze-brown hair, which fell to her shoulders in neat waves. She had honey-brown eyes. She had a dimple on each cheek.

And she had the natural charm to match her physical appearance. Unlike most models, she came across as somewhat introverted, and had a tender, somewhat reserved smile, but made up for it with her naturally fluttering eyes. A natural heartthrob, she would stop a room in its tracks wherever she went, and guys were often left immobilized in her presence – there was indeed good reason to add her to the Seven Wonders of the World.

And I was indeed immobilized as I watched her dancing in the centre of the crowd, red pom-poms waving. I continued to watch as two girls to her side lifted her up by her feet, so she emerged above everyone else.

"And now, stand up and make some noise!" called out the PA announcer. Without thinking, I stood with the hometown fans and began to cheer, as the girls continued their routine. Unable to take my eyes off of her, I continued to applause, forgetting I was on the opposing team. In that moment, the noisy room, the flash of the cameras, they were all gone. I was in the room alone with her.

"The starting lineups for the Los Angeles Clippers," I suddenly heard, "Number 21, Harry Madison."

Taken completely by surprise, I snapped back into reality, stepping forward onto the court, slapping fives with my teammates. I made my way back to the sideline as they continued to read out our lineups, heart beating, nerves tingling at the mere sight of this girl.

Before long, we had taken to the court for the opening tip-off, and I exploded into action. Their centerman managed to tip the ball to his side, but I swiftly swept in to steal the ball, outracing them for an easy lay-up.

For the rest of the game, I had been so perked that I spent the rest of the game rushing by opponents, stealing the ball in the process. I was scoring from all areas of the court, the free-throw line, the paint, or off beyond the arc.

The Heat continued to apply the pressure. They sent defenders after me, but I somehow kept slipping through their fingers. Nothing seemed to work. They tried to block my shots. They tried to steal, they tried to cut off the passing lanes. But I piled on the points. By the end of the third quarter, we were up 90-60.

I returned to the sidelines as the lights dimmed. The spotlights then caught Cherrie sliding across the court in her socks. Stopping center-court, she waved her pom-poms high, and then her fellow cheerleaders slid in behind her, carrying on their routine.

By that moment, I had forgotten completely that she was there to whip up support for the opposing Miami Heat. Caught up in my own euphoria for her, I failed to focus as we took to the court once again.

The next thing I realized, the Heat had somehow found another gear. Somewhat caught off guard, I was unable to keep up as they began to surge past me and my teammates. Before we realized it, they edged past us 110-108.

That crushing collapse, fortunately, served as a wake-up call as we marched through the regular season, taking nobody for granted. Ultimately, we would face the Heat again in the NBA Finals.

Once again, I faced off with Cherrie and her charms. Every time she took to that court, I could not help watching her dance, whipping up the crowds in a frenzy, and leaving me entranced in her spell. I was forced to fight it off and not get distracted.

The Heat continued to come out strong against us, ultimately pushing us to seven games. In the end though, we managed to successfully defend our title.

Three seasons went by before I hit the open market as an unrestricted free agent. During this time, however, we seemed to have hit a plateau, only once reaching the NBA Finals, where we'd lost to Miami.

I was happy to stay in Los Angeles, but Fred advised me to test free agency offers. "You went far, little brother," he had once said. "But you could go further. Hold out a while, if for nothing else, to keep the public in suspense."

I grinned deviously at his suggestion, realizing that I held the public's attention, and could play the market. The Clippers had offered me $120 million over six years, but Fred encouraged me to seek over $20 million per annum. Never did I expect to receive an offer from the Heat.

I remember the ensuing commotion from the press, when I turned down the Clippers' offer. Many were speculating how much I would want to sign for. Others were already anticipating that I would be leaving the Clippers and signing somewhere else. That prospect set the whole basketball world on edge like an unfolding television drama.

I remember Fred receiving numerous offer sheets from as many as five other franchises, including the Lakers, who had offered $145 million over seven years. He told me he would listen in on all offers before selecting the best one.

Halfway into July, I was out surfing just off the shore from my Malibu home. As I was coming in from the surf, I saw Fred come running up into the water, waving his arms.

"I got you a new contract! I got you a new contract!" I heard him shout. I let my board roll in toward him.

"The Miami Heat has offered a contract of $125 million for five years," he said.

I could not believe it. The Miami Heat actually offered me a contract. Here it was, the opportunity to get to be closer to Cherrie, a shot to try my luck.

I also thought about Florida, another place basking in sunshine and a great place to go surfing. It was another lively city with great culture. I could not pass it up.

"Great news, Fred," I said. "Well this fall, I'm taking my talents to South Beach!"

The resulting move, predictably, sent shockwaves throughout the basketball world. People were split over my decision – many were loyal to Clippers and burned me in effigy for leaving. A few had even uttered death threats. But there were many more who thanked me for my seven years in Los Angeles. Others would continue to follow me in Miami.

It was a firestorm all right, but it only helped my image, that I was someone in demand and could sell tickets wherever I went. I have no regrets about leaving Los Angeles, for I was now ready to turn the page.

Chapter 4

OUR SEASON OPENER COULD not have come sooner that fall. All summer long, I had been put through the paces in the most grueling training camp. Coach Herb Carter, a former sergeant with the Marines, was a micromanager and a disciplinarian. I'd never been put through such intensity, even for the Olympics.

He had lined up a very extensive fitness training program, pushing us to the brink. On the court, he was very detailed in on the court plays, on which he constantly drilled us every time we got on the court. Everyone was to play the "Heat way."

I can remember one practice scrimmage before opening night. Despite having been drilled in all of his plays, I could not help but revert to my own style whenever I took to the court. At one point, when I caught a pass from the toss-up, drove through the opposition, and then sinking a one-arm shot following a couple of quick spins. He quickly blew a whistle.

"You should have made a pass on that one, Madison," he barked.

I sighed in frustration. It was a natural play, was he jealous of my abilities or something? The scrimmage continued on, and despite having been drilled continuously over his book, I could not help but revert to my natural freestyle game. I was beginning to regret choosing to Miami, where the grass seemed greener, only to run into a clash with this taskmaster.

Opening night finally arrived against the Cleveland Cavaliers. Feeling frustrated from Carter's rages and challenges over the summer, I was going to take it out on the court, show him what I could do.

The pre-game video began to play overhead, and then flame throwers fired as Cherrie and the cheerleaders emerged onto the court. Seeing her for the first time lifted my spirits and fueled my drive to prove myself.

As the game began, I leapt right into action. Stealing the ball from the opponents, I cut through traffic. As one defender bore down on me, I stepped back and netted my shot.

The rest of the quarter continued to unfold as I confidently poured it on, scoring field goals from all parts of the court. The Cavaliers clearly had no answer for me – and before long my teammates soon, for the most part, they threw their playbook out the window and focused on getting me the ball.

Towards the end of the first quarter, as I saw Cherrie sitting at the sidelines waving her pom-poms, I nearly tripped over myself, catching a pass from one of my teammates, rushing forward and then dunking the ball in the net as time expired.

As Carter rounded us all up to the side of the court and began going over his game plan, the cheerleaders stepped forward and began their dances. I suddenly stopped and turning to the court, I looked for Cherrie in the crowd.

I saw her dancing in the centre of the crowd, swaying her arms sideways as the cheerleaders shouted out their team spirit chant. The girls to her side then lifted her up by her feet, so she emerged above everyone else. Fans recognizing the model gave her a large applause, accompanied by what seemed like a number of whistles.

Realizing my chance, I impulsively stepped onto the court and did a break dance, circling the cheerleaders and chanting along with them. One by one, my teammates followed me onto the court and began free styling, until the whole team was out there. The girls just danced along as though our appearing on court was part of routine. We carried out our routine until the allotted time was up.

Carter was not particularly impressed that I walked out onto the floor. As we moved over to the sidelines, he approached me with a serious look on his face. "What's this business, dancing around with the cheerleaders like a little schoolgirl?" he demanded.

"But it's all about team spirit," I said.

"Are you putting on a show?" he asked. "Or do you want to win?"

"Team spirit brings a win," I said. "The team is hyped up and feels ready to perform."

Coach said nothing at first. He looked up and saw the applause from the audience was growing large. He couldn't argue with me that I got the audience's attention and that the team was ready to go.

"I'll give you one more chance, Madison," he said. "One more antic like this and you're suspended until further notice."

I shrugged and got ready for the next quarter, waving to the applauding fans once more, many of whom replied with several hoots and hollers. "If he really wants to suspend me," I thought, "they are going to object to that." With a sigh of relief, knowing that the fans were on my side, I took my place on the court, ready to show him that I was indispensable.

As the quarter began, I was immediately on the ball, scoring from half court. For the rest of the game, I had been so perked that I spent the rest of the game rushing by opponents, stealing the ball in the process. My teammates seemed to learn to adapt to my presence, as I would consistently guide them across the court to the opponent's net. By the end of the third quarter, we were up 90-60. There was nothing the coach could say about my game now, for the crowd all stood on their feet, cheering wildly.

We kept playing hard, successfully holding off the Cavaliers, and finishing the game with a score of 139-70. By now, my place with the Heat was sealed.

"That's quite a stunt you pulled out there." That was from Phil Johnson, the starting point guard.

By now, we were in the locker room. I was anxiously changing, hoping to catch Cherrie before she disappeared.

"Well," I said, "I guess I have my spontaneous moments. I think it was a good move."

"Yes," he answered, "but with Carter, you don't pull any nonsense like that. It's only because you're our new star that he's not going to touch you, but next time, it's going to be different."

I shrugged. "Okay. So would you have Cherrie's number?"

Phil could only laugh. "No. She never gives out her phone number. In fact, she never hangs out with anyone, save for two girls on the squad. She's quite reclusive."

I sighed. "Wow, we can get this close to her," I said, "but we're still so far." By now, I was fully dressed and ready to go.

"Good luck trying to get five minutes of her time," was all Phil could say as I hurried out the door. For once, it seemed that I could no longer rely on heroism to fish for love, at least from this one elusive fish, the biggest one ever.

The month carried on. Day in and day out, I would show up to practices. Every weekend, I would attend parties with many of my teammates held at our personal residences.

Game nights came and went: I'd come in, drive the lanes, set up plays, and place the ball in the net pretty much every way I knew how. I tried many new tricks on the court, during practice and in games, and found new ways to beat the opponents. This seemed to give the fans a new thrill, as I gradually became the talk of the town more and more. Fans out of town likewise were interested in my game, and opposing arenas were often filled to capacity whenever we came to down. The opponents, well, they seemed out of luck, not having any more clues on how to stop me and we continued to rack up our wins.

I attended numerous team functions, appeared in numerous publicity photo shoots, gave several after-game television interviews, and even appeared in several television commercials, promoting both Miami Heat and other businesses asking for my endorsements. The ever-present flash of the publicity photo shots were getting more and more prevalent.

As it was in Los Angeles, I could not go anywhere in public without fans stopping me, asking for autographs or pictures. Many of them expressed their excitement at a potential NBA dynasty here in Miami, and were proudly cheering us toward a championship. Once, while passing by an outdoor basketball court, several youths playing there dropped their game, asking for my autograph and begging me to show them some of my tricks.

Outside of basketball, I opened restaurants out here in Miami, and the business thrived more than ever. I continued my endorsements with Nike and several other businesses, both local and nation-wide enterprises. I appeared in more publicity photo shoots and television commercials than I did while in California.

Things normally don't get much better than this. I had it made: I was making very big bucks and could pretty much come and go as I please, do whatever I like day in and day out. I had bought a nice waterfront home in South Beach, a new Porsche, plus a couple of pleasure craft. But in my new world down here, there was something missing that kept it from being the perfect world I know it could be. It was not hard to realize what that missing piece was. Or rather, who it was.

It was no one other than Cherrie Lopez-Harrison. Back in Los Angeles, I had dated numerous other beautiful celebrities, mostly fashion models or Hollywood actresses. My relationships were great while they lasted, but for one reason or another, they never lasted long. "Oh well," I often told myself, "there's always a bigger fish." After Cherrie, however, there simply wasn't a bigger fish to catch.

As the days had gone by, Cherrie had become my fancy. I collected numerous posters and publicity photos of her, placing them all over different walls in my house. During game time, I was energized seeing Cherrie dancing on the court before I got up to play, and having her in the same room only energized me to play harder.

I'd always tried to catch her after games, sometimes, anxiously counting off the last seconds of the games, so I could take off. But I was always slowed down by Coach's locker room discussions and the post-game press interviews. Every time I got out of the locker room, Cherrie was always gone.

I'd left notes for her with several other cheerleaders on the squad. Normally, whenever any of the players left a note for a cheerleader, they would hear back from her on short notice, and most of the girls would quickly accept an invitation to a party or even a brief outing. But try as I may, I never heard back from her. She was elusive like a unicorn.

Before long, I decided I would try to get hold of her phone number. That, I knew, would be very difficult, because she only hung out with three girls on the squad. I wondered how I could go about my task, and then realized I possibly could ask out one of the three girls on a date, make them comfortable around me, and try and smuggle out her number.

The opportunity came when I ran into one of those girls in the hallway after the game. Karen Buchannan, also another model on the catwalk and an aspiring pop singer.

"Hey Karen," I called out to her, "how does it?"

She turned and smiled. "Harry Madison," she greeted me, "nice game today. You've really given the team a new edge."

"I hope you're excited as I am," I responded, approaching her. "It's been a real blast down here in Sunshine State. I'm prepared to turn up the heat and set the world on fire here when we win."

"Well that sure is bound to happen," she agreed as we turned and walked down the hallway. "No one can beat us now that we've got Molokai Express to sweep it all away."

I laughed again. "Yeah, so what are you up to this evening?" I asked her.

"Well normally, I'd get together with some of the girls after game time, but today, everyone else has other functions. Cherrie had to catch a flight to Virginia, Julie's gone up to Orlando, Amy's got a date, and I'm here."

"Aww, so are you all alone tonight?" I stopped and then beamed toward her. "Hey care to go out for a drink?"

"Sure," she responded. "You know, I haven't had dinner yet. Been busy all day."

"Good, I could do for a bite myself. Have you ever been to the new Harry's across the street?"

"No. Is that your restaurant? Let's go there."

We walked out and headed down to my new sports bar across the street from the arena, my first location in Florida. The place was alive, as many fans, having just come from watching the game themselves, had gathered here for an after-game drink or snack. Televisions mounted throughout the bar showed recaps from our game as well as other sporting events.

As we came inside, I was stopped by numerous fans wanting to congratulate me on the win. Karen held onto my left arm as I gave out several autographs while we made our way through the crowd and sat at the bar. We ordered a couple burgers and drinks.

Throughout the night, people kept coming up to us. Several people also recognized Karen and asked for her autograph. We had several drinks when Karen began singing out pop songs. Clearly, she was beginning to get drunk from the booze.

"For the Heat and their run to the championship," she began and several other patrons listened in. "And Harry the Molokai Express to lead the way."

She broke into song, singing out a popular tune and people listened in. Some began snapping their fingers in beat to her music, and singing along with her. Even I began humming to her music.

I've heard her singing at times when passing their locker room. She does have a beautiful voice, but at this time, after three or four drinks, she was off tune. Still, after having downed several drinks myself, I was in the mood to follow along with her music. I gulped down the last of the stuff in my bottle and hummed along. By now, a circle of patrons had formed around us, following along with her.

I don't remember what time we left the bar, but after a few more songs from Karen, I put my arm around her and accompanied her out, to a round of applause. We waved goodbye to everyone in there.

It was then when I asked her for Cherrie's number, and Karen, loose-tongued from the drinks, gave me the number. I punched it right away into my mobile phone, as we hailed down a taxi.

I awoke the next morning, feeling a hangover from the previous night. I pulled myself out of bed and hopped into the shower. Water splashed into my face, waking me up, and suddenly, I realized we were leaving on a five-game road trip that afternoon.

Hopping out of the shower, I quickly got dressed and quickly packed for the trip, before hopping into the car and driving down to the arena for an early practice before we departed.

In the back of my mind, I was alive with excitement, knowing that I had Cherrie's number safely in my phone. I could not call her up right away, but I made a point to call sometime during the trip.

Shortly after arriving in Dallas, I whipped out my phone and tried to call Cherrie right away. I waited for almost a minute as the phone rang.

To my utter surprise, a man's voice answered.

"Hello?"

"Hello?" I greeted. "Is Cherrie there?"

"Cherrie? I'm sorry you got the wrong number. This is..."

I hung up in disgust. So much for bragging about having her number. She's become elusive as the wind.

The days dragged on by. Back in Florida, during games, I often tried to get her attention. Following the games, I'd rushed off to catch her, once even avoiding the press for the post-game interview. Once, I'd seen her walking down the street with some friends. Just as I tried to run across the street, several basketball fans stopped me for autographs. By the time I had been done with them, she was gone.

Pursuing Cherrie had depleted me physically and emotionally. I had suffered many sleepless nights consumed with the hunger to complete my world and to somehow find the elusive missing piece. I had been staring up at my wall of her pictures and whenever I lay down to sleep, I could do nothing but dream of her.

These nights had left me haggard and unfocused the following mornings. During practice, I was unable to keep in step, and often had been made to do extra laps, normally a simple feat, had I not had so many sleepless nights. My play began to suffer during game time, and consequently, I took plenty of heat from Coach Carter, particularly after one loss.

"Welcome to the real world, young man," he had yelled at me while in the dressing room after the game. "You got to earn your place, by learning your place. We will see what you are made of."

I had been benched the following game. Right away, the fans seemed to side with me, and many of them had burned Coach Carter in effigy for sitting me out, booing him right from the start of the game. I took comfort in their support, but nothing could cover up my disappointment.

Despite the setbacks and frustrations, I shook myself off, vowing to get up and find her somehow. Someday, I was going to catch her, make her mine, and kiss the dark days goodbye.

Chapter 5

AN OPPORTUNITY FINALLY came when I was invited to MC a fashion show at our arena about a couple weeks later, where multiple fashion houses, including the one owned by Cherrie's mother, were presenting. I was surprised to be invited to speak, since I've never presented before, but I gladly obliged, knowing that she would be there to present her ware.

The week leading up to the event, I had been rehearsing every day for several hours at a time. I hadn't done a presentation since doing speech class in high school, and had to be refreshed on some of the basics of public speaking.

But when the day arrived, I felt at home as I came onstage to a grand applause from the audience, with spotlights shining down on me. I waved to the crowd and shook a couple of hands. I was beaming from ear to ear as I made my announcement.

"Ladies and gentlemen," I announced, "welcome to our seventh annual presentation of Heat Wave fashion wear, sponsored by American Airlines and your very own Miami Heat."

I continued to list off the different events for the evening, before the show was finally underway, and the models came walking out from the entrance. I would stay at the front of the stage, gesturing back toward the models as they came out, describing their outfits.

There were several models who had come to present before Cherrie made her first appearance. I can still recall the flipping in my heart as she came along, wearing a violet dress with a row of diamonds around the neckline.

"Ladies and gentlemen," I announced above the rising applause as we made our way forward, "the Lopez-Harrison flagship, a one-of-a-kind silk one-piece gown. Set to be released this fall, it is a limited edition. Retails at $25,000."

I watched her as she waved somewhat shyly at the crowd with a flutter in her eyes, before twirling and making her way back to the door. I could hear a few whistles from the crowd, and I laughed inside.

The remaining three hours of the show flew by quickly. Several more models had come along, and Cherrie herself made three more appearances. She came out later wearing athletic wear, and later she posed in casual wear, jeans and a blouse. She wore a different evening dress on her last appearance. Every time she came out, I noticed the camera flash rapidly going off across the room, for she garnered more attention than anyone else.

Before I realized it, it was all over, and it was time to disembark. I went back into the locker room, returned the microphone and equipment, before washing off my face, for I had been sweating with nervousness and excitement.

As I came out of the locker room and was passing down the hallway, I saw her just coming out of the women's locker room ahead of me.

"Cherrie," I called to her, and she turned and looked my direction.

"Oh, hi," she said, somewhat shyly as I came alongside her and looked her directly in those beautiful brown eyes which fluttered somewhat. Inside, my heart skipped a beat, but I caught hold of myself.

"You weren't rushing off so soon were you?" I asked.

"No, no thank goodness, I don't have to make a midnight ride tonight," she replied. "I actually have to go to my mother's booth, make more public appearances."

"Are you nervous?"

"Oh, yes," Cherrie answered. "It's one thing to be up on the catwalk or on the stage, but I freak out when I step into the crowds.

I fear someone may mug me or something. In fact, can I hold onto your hand?"

This was the moment I was waiting for, and one I'll never forget. I took her by those buttery-soft hands of hers and led her out through the door into the public area. I could feel her pulse racing wildly with apparent nervousness. Mine was racing too, with sheer excitement.

Almost instantly, upon emerging into the public area, we were greeted by the flashing of cameras from both the press and individual attendees. The flashings effectively lit the whole room as we tried to make our way through the crowd. Cherrie gripped my hand tighter. I was beaming from ear to ear as we went along with this doll of a girl.

The whole length of the corridors had different booths where fashion houses represented on the catwalk could talk to the press and present their ware. Eventually, we made it to her mother's booth, where she was with some of her assistant designers and executives. They were busily answering questions from reporters who surrounded them.

"Here she comes, the girl of the hour!" one of the reporters when Cherrie and I arrived there. Right away, they had us pose for what they all claimed were cover page for their respective magazines. I grinned broadly, knowing this was my chance I had been waiting for.

"Well, well, if it isn't Molokai Express," her mother chimed in, looking at us.

"This one's for the books." That was from another woman.

"Hello ladies," I greeted them.

Cherrie suddenly released my hand, and jumped into her mother's arms, before turning and grinning innocently at the press for more photos. They then turned back to me as their people continued handling questions from the press.

It was but ten short minutes with her, but it was enough to fuel my hope that somehow, I knew I was going to eventually get to her and have my moment. That glimmer of hope was a breath of fresh air and for the first time in a long time, I began to feel like my normal self.

That next day, we had a game at home. As I made my way out from the locker room, I smiled and waved at Cherrie sitting on the end zone, and I saw her smile back at me.

At that moment, the announcer called for everyone to stand at attention for the national anthem, after which, all the cheerleaders emerged onto the court and the announcer began announcing the starting lineups.

"A guard, standing six-foot three, number 21, Harry 'Molokai Express' Madison," he said, when he got to my name. As I made my way out onto center court, I saw Cherrie, standing up on the extended hands of a male cheerleader, do a back flip right overhead, landing feet first onto the hands of another cheerleader, and then point down at me.

At that moment, my heart racing with excitement and determination, for I had my moment with her, and now, I was one step closer to completing my world. And so, today I would return to my former self, and this time, I would play harder than ever for Cherrie Lopez-Harrison.

On the initial tossup, I took the pass from centerman Jimmy Carter, rushed through the opponents single-handedly, and quickly released a shot from the three-point zone while their power forward was bearing down on me. Thump! The ball went into the net.

I was back. My play before tonight had been adequate, as I worked my way back into Coach Carters' graces. But tonight, I had exploded into action once again, employing various tricks and techniques, some of which I had virtually improvised on the spot. But no matter how unorthodox my game, it worked, and we quickly mounted our lead.

I recalled several plays where I had leapt after the ball and made single-handed passes seemingly into the middle of nowhere. A teammate would grab the ball and find himself in good scoring position, and of course he scored. Other times, I had shot a basket from half-court.

But for me, I was just so wrapped up with playing for Cherrie, that I forgot completely about the score and was focused on driving hard, as if we were down 30 points.

At the end of the match, having won the game 140-80, I was immediately engulfed by the press. I took a moment to answer all their questions, but soon hurried off to catch Cherrie. I found her out in the parkade, still dressed in her cheerleader's garb. She turned when I called out to her.

"Cherrie, hey are you off so soon?" I called.

"Oh, hey there," she replied. "Yeah, there's nothing else left going on, so I'm just about to go home. Why, what's going on?"

"Oh, I just never see you around," I responded. "Promised I'd try and catch you one of these days. Hey, I've got a little housewarming party in a couple days. I'm inviting everyone to come. Can you make it?"

Cherrie stopped in her tracks. "Oh, no you're not another guy trying to catch me alone," she said. "I get too many of those."

"I'm sorry if I'd scared you off."

"Well, I don't mind parties, but I've had so many guys try to make advances. That scares me off. That's why I get nervous in public."

"Hey, hey," I replied. "I think it's not fair that every eye is on you this way. Calling someone 'most beautiful woman in the world,' now that is just too much pressure for one girl. It invites such unwanted attention."

"Yeah," Cherrie went on, turning and walking over to her car. I stayed with her. "So how can I know that you're not trying to follow me? What next?"

"Come now, girl. Okay, okay, I'm sorry. I shouldn't have said I'd try and catch you. I didn't mean that. If I'd offended you..."

"No, it's okay," Cherrie interrupted. "I just overreacted. I'm scared of guys in general, that's all." As she climbed into her car, she added, "I might make it to your party though. Thanks for inviting me. Well I'm out of here." She started her engine and revved it up, before she pulled out and drove off.

As I turned and headed back to the dressing room to change out of my jersey, I felt myself tingling with excitement. I finally caught Cherrie alone for a few minutes, but she opened up to me. I knew it was only a matter of time before I would woo her over and she could be mine. I wanted her to be mine, and I would do whatever it took.

Suddenly, my thoughts were interrupted when I ran into Jimmy in the hallway. "Hey dude, how are the party planning coming along?" he asked.

"Well, I just tried to send an invite to the guest of honour, Cherrie Lopez-Harrison."

"Haha, there you go again," Jimmy laughed. "Good luck trying to get her to come to this party. I've invited her to different functions, and she never shows up, except maybe to one event. She doesn't trust us enough."

"Yeah," I replied. "But she did trust me once to guide her through the crowd."

"Well, you were probably the only guy there."

"I was."

"Then there's the bad news. She'll trust you once, and then she'll avoid you like the plague. I once helped her to a gas station when her car ran out. She thanked me then, but hasn't talked to me since."

"Things are going to be different this time," I said confidently. "I know my way with women. She just needs to be softened up and made to feel comfortable."

"Yeah, but I wouldn't try your tricks on her," Jimmy replied. "You know her boyfriend is a Navy SEAL."

I stopped for a moment and then said, "She's got a boyfriend? Well I've seen girls date one guy for a time, and then move on. I'm going to convince her to move on."

"And when she moves on from you?"

"Fifteen minutes."

I held the party at my home the next evening, as scheduled. I had the whole team over, from my teammates and cheerleading squad to our coaching and management staff. I had my family and some of my friends back from California. But there was no show of Cherrie Lopez-Harrison.

I was not alone in noticing her absence. We were out back, playing some basketball in my rear courtyard. As I was resting on the sidelines, my brother Fred joined me.

"Hey dude," he began, "where's that angel with whom you appeared on the cover of People's Magazine?"

"I don't know," I said. "I'd invited her, but she's just playing hard to get."

Fred chuckled. "Oh boy," he responded, "you're really going for that big fish. What about your sweetheart at home?"

"Always plenty of fish in the sea. Always a new challenge I'll have to meet."

"Surely you're not serious."

"Yes I am. And don't call me Shirley."

The rest of the evening carried on. We continued to play some more basketball in the court. We went surfing out on the beach. We had more activities inside.

Later that evening, we were gathering in the foyer, which served as a formal reception hall. People were chatting with one another over their drinks, when suddenly the front door opened and in strode John Hoover, the team owner. Accompanying him, arm in arm, was Cherrie's mother. In tow, I saw Cherrie herself.

"Ladies and gentlemen," Mr. Hoover announced over the chatter. "We apologize for our tardiness, but I have a surprise announcement." The crowd fell silent and looked on them.

"This was a quick turn of events, but Marie Lopez-Harrison and I are engaged."

It was certainly a surprise to nearly everyone in the room. For a second, the crowd was silently stunned, and then applause swept the room. Respectfully, I came up and shook his hand, then hers, congratulating them on their engagement. The rest of the evening, people were coming up and congratulating them, chattering excitedly over life together.

Meanwhile, I tried to find Cherrie again, but she somehow disappeared in the crowd. It wasn't hard, given the number of people in the room.

"Amazing," I had said to myself. "How can a person not find someone in his own house?"

She had disappeared again like an elusive shadow. But despite the initial fruitlessness, I knew deep down inside, I was going to overcome the final barrier and break through to her.

Chapter 6

I FINALLY BEGAN TO receive my dream for Christmas that year. The week before Christmas, I'd been surfing just off the beachside near my home. Wading in from the surf, I saw Cherrie playing volleyball with some of her friends out on the beach and confidently strode up to them. One of the girls looked up and saw me coming.

"Hey, it's the Molokai Express," she said. "What's up dude?"

"Been out enjoying the surf," I said. "It's nice down here in Florida. Hey, can I play?"

"Yes, we're honored you could join us. You join our team, we're outmatched. We'll rotate you in if we get the ball."

"Thanks," I said, sidling up to the side of the court. "Volleyball and basketball are really quite similar. You jump and knock a ball around."

As the opposing girl delivered her serve, the girl nearest to me bumped the ball forward. Cherrie, who was on my side, leapt up and tipped the ball over for a successful kill.

"There," she said. "Let's see what the Molokai Express can do."

I tossed the ball up, but being somewhat excited, I served it a little too hard. The ball flew far past the end of the court, bounced off a pavement, and rolled into a parking lot.

"Oops," I said. "Hyper-overkill."

Some of the girls laughed. "This is volleyball, not NBA," another girl jabbed.

"Awesome shot though," Cherrie chimed in.

I ran to fetch the ball. I saw it roll right through a group of parked cars. I just managed to catch up to it, just before it rolled out into the street.

The girls were gone from the court by the time I got back. For a moment my heart sank disappointedly, until I heard someone call out, "Com'on Cherrie, you can do it!"

I looked up and there were the girls further out on the beach, watching some surfboarders out on the wake. Looking into the distance, I saw Cherrie sailing into an oncoming wave.

I realized quickly that Cherrie was bound for trouble. Having expensive surfing experience, I knew the incoming wave looked like it could swell as high as ten or fifteen feet. And Cherrie, obviously an inexperienced surfboarder, being crouched on her hands and knees, would be swamped easily.

"No!" I shouted, taking off down the beach. "She's going to drown!" I threw myself into the water, in time to see the wave swell higher, Cherrie struggling to hang on.

I swam out at full strength, my eyes stung shut by the salty seawater as I glided two feet below the surface. But even underwater, I could hear a scream from the beach.

"No! Oh, no, Cherrie!"

She was likely dumped over, head down. In shallow water, she could hit her head on the sand. In deep water, the force of an unexpected plunge could drive her down and drown her.

A surfboard skimmed by overhead unmanned, followed by the crashing wave driving for the beach. Obviously the one Cherrie had been riding. Pulling myself upwards, I poked my head out of the water and looked around. In the crystal-clear water, I could see Cherrie indeed having been plunged underwater almost five feet below the surface, I plunged down again in her direction stretching my arms outward.

I grabbed Cherrie and arched my way to the surface again. Flipping her onto my back, I swam back to shore at full strength, until I reached shallow water. I stood up, threw the girl onto my shoulder and carried her ashore.

Cherrie was not breathing. I gently set her on the beach, as her friends rushed up around her.

"Oh, my baby!" Just now I recognized her mother, as she suddenly crouched down and took her daughter into her arms, clapping at her back.

The whole scene slowly blurred into view. Just now, I recognized her two friends from the squad. I recognized her aunt, whom I'd met at the catwalk. But there were four other girls there whom I did not recognize.

Everyone crowded around the girl, who'd lost colour in her face. They clapped her back and chest and slapped at her face. Her mother even performed a Heinrich maneuver on her daughter. Eventually, she coughed up water and the colour returned to her face.

Her mother rushed up and threw her arms around me. "Thank you so much, Harry," she cried. "You saved my daughter's life."

"Lifeguard Harry!" That was from one of Cherrie's young friends on the squad. "You really are the real thing, and not just another cheerleader."

Meanwhile, Cherrie, slightly dazed, looked around at the commotion. "What happened?" she asked weakly.

"Molokai Express here had saved your life," one of her friends replied. "You took a real bad plunge out there."

She gently sat up. "It was scary out there. I didn't realize how high that wave could swell. I thought I was a goner."

"Yeah," I responded, "we wouldn't want to lose you so soon." I picked up my board and added, "Any time you like, why don't I show you how the pros do it?"

This would ultimately prove to be my breakthrough moment, for Cherrie relaxed and smiled at me. I knew that she was opening up to me. "Sure thing," she replied. "I would love to go surfing one of these days."

News of the surfing incident made television and magazines for the coming weeks. We were invited to appear together on numerous specialty programs and talk shows. It was sensational news, how the Heat's new superstar had single-handedly rescued Ms. Eighth Wonder of the World. Marketers soon capitalized on this by having us do photo shoots together, and I began to see our pictures on magazine covers.

I remember appearing in an exclusive 20/20 interview with her. We were called in to the studio down in Florida, where the host sat us down and asked us about what had been happening.

"I had decided to try surfing and finding his board," she had begun. "I went out onto the surf with the board, thinking the waves were manageable."

I looked at her the whole time she was speaking, noticing her trembling expressions as she recounted her story.

"I often go surfing in my spare time," I had said, "I knew about the surf and I knew she was bound for trouble."

"I got by a medium-sized wave," she went on, "and I thought I was progressing smoothly, and then the huge wave swelled up in front of me, and I had no idea what to do in that instance. I was knocked out instantly and the next thing I knew, I had been choking up."

"I saw her go under," I was saying. "She was plunged perhaps ten feet down into the water, and I had to swim down to fetch her out. I had done some water safety training, but I am no professional lifeguard. It was a brush of good luck, this mission."

The host went on to talk about the nature of surfing and the importance of safety on the water. Later segments showed other people being interviewed while out on the beach. A few people had claimed to have seen the rescue, but they didn't realize the characters involved in the rescue.

"It is a brush with death for the Eighth Wonder, Cherrie Lopez-Harrison, but it took the bold heroics of Molokai Express Harry Madison to rescue her and bring her back to safety," the hostess concluded.

Cherrie and I went on our first date that evening, following our interview. We went to my beachside location South Beach, not far from where I lived. The place was bustling as usual, and the whole place was stirring when we stepped inside. Patrons with cameras or camera phones stopped to take our pictures, and I waved to them. A number of fans had come up to ask for autographs.

"I should thank you again for saving my life," she had said. "Two times, you had helped me out. Back during the Heat wave show and then out on the ocean."

I looked into those beautiful brown eyes, now softening up. She was gradually engaging me, opening up and letting me into her life. I beamed at her, eager to reach in and be there for her.

"It has been so lonely," she went on, "being here alone without my boyfriend. He is always busy up in Virginia, when he is not out on the field. He only ever gets one week off the whole year. It's frightening to face life alone, and I need all the support I can get."

I paused for a moment and listened to her, taken in by her elegant beauty and gentle demeanor. Inside, my heart was flipping. I reached over and poured her some wine from the bottle on the table.

"I hope I won't get into trouble if I'm serving a minor," I said.

"Thanks." She blushed at my humour and her eyes fluttered again. I knew she was of age, but a lot of underage girls easily can pass for early twenties.

"It is my pleasure to reach out and give you a hand whenever you need," I went on. "Life is tough, and it's not fair when you have to face it alone."

"I am a lost girl," she replied. "I had faced so much in my early life, and at this stage, being me, it is the hardest thing in the world."

I sighed as I looked into her eyes, now showing a glimmer of fear. All the more, I wanted to be there for her. I reached over and took her by the hand. She accepted that and smiled back at me.

Being in the spotlight with this angel of a girl only fueled every bone in my body with excitement. That was evident the following evening, when we played the Indianapolis Racers.

It was my best game of my career, a 90-point, 13-assist effort. The whole time, I had been flying across the court, not only driving hard to the net, but I was also making some difficult plays at both ends of the court. This game, I even improvised new tricks, like a one-hand back-toss or a volleyball bump or set, moves that still worked as my "unique passes" caught a few open teammates. Once, I've even scored on a sudden back throw from just in the half-court line. It was evident from the reactions from the stands that everyone was amazed to watch me on this roll. The flabbergasted opponents did not know how to stop me, and we easily won 194-120.

I was soon engulfed by the press while on the court. They were not only interested in tonight's game, but were eager to cover my unfolding relationship with Cherrie, who was promptly brought over for a photo shoot.

I was riding high with excitement, but the wind was soon taken out of my sail, when Jimmy approached me in the locker room with a message from Coach Carter. "Hey, good game tonight, Harry," he began, "but Coach is starting to have some issues. He says that you are starting to push the limit out there."

The smile on my face slipped away. "What does he expect? We won the game."

"We won, but you are not falling in step with the book," he continued. "Coach asked me to speak to you. He is warning you to stop your risk taking game and play more within the team system." He soon looked more serious. "Is it about Cherrie?" he asked. "Is that why you were on such a roll?"

"Why, of course," I responded.

"Dude, I hate to say this, but I really think this girl is getting to your head and messing up your judgement. Things are not going to last forever on this hot streak of yours. Soon she will leave and you will crash and burn, and hurt yourself, as well as the rest of us."

I was shocked at his words, but I picked myself up again. I had a date that night with Cherrie, so I showered and changed quickly, before going out to join her.

We then went out to my new beachside grill, a new outdoor location on Coconut Grove We picked up an order of fish and chips and sat down by the beach. A number of fans stopped by and asked us for autographs and pictures, but before long, we had time to ourselves.

"You wouldn't believe it," I said, "but the coach has gone and given me a lecture, even despite this being my best game yet and none of the guys backed me up." I talked to her about what had been happening in the locker room.

"Oh, that's not fair," she replied.

"Yeah, well, I guess that they are mostly jealous over you," I continued. "Nobody expected that we would be going on a date together. If I hadn't been there to save you, that wouldn't happen."

She smiled. "No, they are jealous over your game," she said, and cracked up in laughter and I laughed with her. "I do owe you my life, though," she continued. "Now if only they can let you play as you will. Ted, well he says that you got to give credit where credit is due."

I gulped. She is still hanging onto him. I haven't got her yet. But I would continue to make an effort to breakthrough, just as I have done on the court. I gazed longingly into her eyes, taking in the pounding surf before we dug into our food.

Chapter 7

MR. HOOVER'S WEDDING took place on Valentines' Day. To my surprise, he had invited me to accompany him as one of his groomsmen, along with Jimmy, Phil, and Coach Carter, plus several of his own relatives. I took this invitation as a token for strengthening our respective business relationship.

The wedding took place at a cathedral just outside of the city. In attendance were numerous prominent businesspeople from the Miami area, many of whom were business associates of Mr. Hoover and Ms. Lopez-Harrison, along with the entire team and their families.

Outside, members of the local press gathered to photograph VIPs in attendance, as well as Ms. Lopez-Harrison for when she arrived with her train of bridesmaids. Her own daughter Cherrie was her maid of honour.

When she finally entered, everyone gaped at how striking she looked in her flowing gown, which she herself had personally designed. But try as she may, even in her gown, she could not match her daughter's unmatchable beauty.

Following the ceremony, which lasted over an hour, they held a buffet aboard a cruise ship owned by Mr. Hoover's company. It was during this event when I finally chose to pop the question.

I ran into Cherrie as I wandered through the place. We made our way back toward the punchbowl, talking to some of the other guests as we went along. As I drew a drink for her, I reached into my pocket and, pulling out a small ring box, I presented it to her.

"To Cherrie, the apple of my eye and product of my dreams," I said to her, as I got down on my knee and extended it to her.

Cherrie looked down at me, hand across her chest, blushing.

"Oh, oh how sweet of you," she responded. She took the box lovingly and opened it.

The others standing there were gaping widely as she pulled out the ring. It was a 90-karat sapphire set amongst a circle of diamonds of varying colours, set on a ring of solid gold. She looked at it, then back up at me.

"Please marry me," I continued. "I wish to spend the rest of my life with you."

For a while, she was speechless. The others around her murmured with surprise and wonder, having witnessed the Cherrie Lopez-Harrison faced with a marriage proposal. She looked on, somewhat dazed. She then turned and wandered off.

Still under the influence of the alcohol, I just began laughing. The others began laughing with me.

"Oh, how to play hard to get," one of them chuckled.

"You sure know how to go out and get 'em," someone else chimed in. "Lay on for the big catch."

"Oh, yeah," I began, "we'll see you back in the chapel soon, from the altar."

Everyone continued to crack up laughing. One guy raised his glass.

"I propose a toast," he announced, "to Harry the Molokai Express on his engagement and marriage to soon to be Mrs. Cherrie Madison."

Word of my proposal spread amongst everyone in attendance. Many of them had even seen Cherrie with the ring. Mr. Hoover himself had even been making jokes about becoming a father-in-law on his wedding day.

I found Cherrie up in the ballroom overlooking the promenade deck chattering excitedly to her friends about how during her mother's wedding, she receives a marriage proposal of her own.

"I'm not supposed to have even been born yet," she laughed. "Am I in the right time?"

"Yeah," someone else added, "whoa man, you're a time traveler!"

Everyone crackled up in laughter, until Cherrie turned and saw me right there. She dropped her glass.

"Hey, I was wondering when you'd show up," she said. "We were just about to have a ball."

"I was wondering where you went," I responded.

"I was telling the world that we were getting married."

"And I was..."

Just then, the attendants were removing tables, leaving an open space on the court. Next thing I knew, everyone was escorted toward the sidelines before the music began to play. Mr. Hoover took his new wife into his arms and began to prance onto the dance floor. For several minutes, it was just the two of them, dancing alone, before other couples filed onto the floor.

I took Cherrie by the arm and led her out onto the floor. She giggled as I put my arm around her, and then gently swept her off her feet. I spun with her and gently set her down, held her close, and brought her nose-to-nose with me. We continued to prance gracefully, vaguely aware of others looking on at us.

I felt I was practically floating; I was on top of the world with her, that I suddenly pulled her close to kiss her. Cherrie suddenly spun, arms outstretched. Letting go of my hand, she proceeded to perform a ballet spin around me, swinging her legs high. She jumped and spun, and then, taking my other hand, she spun herself close to me. I brought her close for a kiss.

I woke up the next morning to find myself alone. "Was I dreaming? Did all these events really take place?" I sighed and pulled myself out of bed, stumbled over to the bathroom, splashing some water on my face. The sudden coldness startled me with a shiver and I looked up into the mirror with a start. I noticed my eyes were bloodshot.

As I got dressed, I looked up at the pictures of Cherrie with a sigh, and then heading downstairs I went out and got into my car to get to our morning practice. As I drove along I picked up my phone and called her.

To my horror, a man's voice answered on the other end. "Hello?" I slammed my phone shut with disgust. Of course, Karen had given me the wrong phone number.

I had come so close, and yet I was so far. In my dream, Cherrie was right there. She was but an optical illusion at the corner of your eye that disappeared when I turned to look. When I reached for her, she vanished like the morning mist. I shuddered as I continued onward slowly realizing the truth.

My day wouldn't get much better when I showed up for practice. Coach Carter was waiting for me in the locker room, alone.

"Hope you enjoyed your night, young man," he said with a warning undertone. "Don't want no more bull on the court like last night, partying up like a drunken animal." Motioning to the floor, he told me to do push ups.

"How many?" I asked.

"Didn't say how many," he replied grimly. I got down on the floor and got started.

I stumbled a bit at first, but soon caught my balance and got working. Before long, a few other guys came into the room, and saw me there on the floor, working like some lowly athlete. I was humiliated, but I kept pushing myself to endure.

After what seemed like an eternity, Coach finally told me to get up again. By now, my arms were sore. "My arms are stiff," I said.

"Don't be a crybaby," he snapped. "You know how to stretch."

I stretched my arms outward and proceeded to do some of the stretch exercises that he taught us.

"If I had Cherrie," I thought to myself, "I would be his boss' son-in-law, and he would not get away with this." I picked up a basketball and then joined the guys outside, who were already in progress with the assigned drills. "She'll be here for tonight's game," I went on. "All will be okay when I see her."

That evening however, Cherrie was not there when we came out into the court. I pinched myself and scanned the squad. Every girl was present, except for her. My heart sunk into despair and nothing could energize me, not even the large applause from the crowd when they announced my name for the starting lineup.

Unable to concentrate, I began to fall apart. On the initial tossup, Jimmy passed me the ball, which struck my face. Startled, I grabbed it and then ran, tripping once, but recovering.

I made a quick pass, and then heard a shriek, followed by a startled expression from the crowd, for I suddenly realized I passed to an opponent. I turned and ran after him as he drove for the net. I leapt in front of him arms outstretched, right as he was making a shot. I managed to make a flying block, but my body then crashed into him, drawing a foul.

The guy would be awarded three free-throw attempts on that play. I shook myself as we gathered around the net and he took his shots, making two baskets.

I pinched myself, as the play continued. I caught the ball, and then deking around an opponent, I turned and made a three point shot, a small redemption for my initial blunder.

Even though I was visibly dogged by my emotions, I managed to carry on for the rest of the game. My play was unspectacular, but adequate enough, for we won the game.

Regardless, Carter would seize on this game to tell me off before the rest of the team in the locker room. "How does it feel now, Mr. Showman?" he had barked at me. "Are you still able to carry that world on your shoulders? Huh?"

He marched over to the chalkboard. "Yeah, that's right," he remarked sarcastically. "Nobody can figure out Molokai Express. Mr.

Too-Good-for-Coach, above the law, the guy who does it all can carry the whole team."

This time, I could only hang my head for I had indeed fallen and he had proceeded to tear into me as a wolf tears into its fallen opponent following the final kill.

"Party animal thinks he can get away with anything, huh boys?" he continued, looking to the rest of the guys, who said nothing, but inside, they could not disagree with him.

After taking a shower and getting changed, I caught a glimpse of a magazine lying on the bench, and I saw it, a picture of my kissing Cherrie while dancing. Splashed on the front headline, "Florida's Favourite Son and Daughter Make out at Parents' Wedding." I sighed and hung my head as I walked out of the room.

The weeks carried on, but time would not heal the wounds. My mind was so wrapped up with the girl, it continued to bog me down to the point when my game went from adequate to sloppy and began to hurt the team.

Before long, the press began to talk about my slump and for the first time in my career, they began to criticize my game.

"He takes so many risks out on the court, I thought it was a wonder he could do what he did," one pundit had remarked. "But he's proof that cockiness does not work."

I expected Carter would bench me, but to my surprise, he never did. He continued to send me out onto the court. I managed to set Cherrie aside for a short time whenever I got on the court, but somehow, I was broken down to mortal status. My tricks no longer worked, and it was only hurting the team.

I soon began to hear opposing fans jeering me whenever we were on the road. "Kryptonite!" I would hear some fans shout.

"Where's your mama?" others would jeer.

"Who's washed up?"

I slowly realized that Coach continued to play me to humiliate me, knowing that I was off my game. Time and again, I tried to get up and prove my critics wrong, but I could not lift the burdens off my shoulders. Before long, I was being booed and jeered at home in Miami as our team began to sink in the standings. I was growing more and more frustrated as I tried to regain my form, but I was finding myself losing even the fans' respect.

I had come home one night, following one particularly brutal home game, where we lost 90-75 to my former team, the Clippers. Coming inside, I made my way to the kitchen where my brother Fred sat around the bar. "Finally hit the wall, have you?" he began. There was sympathy in his voice. "There was a brutal loss tonight."

I moved over to the bar and whipped out a bottle of beer. I popped the cap off and took a swig.

"I have been falling for an illusion," I replied. "She was never here. I was caught chasing the wind."

"Yeah," he replied. "Well, I don't know what to say."

By now, I had hit my breaking point. "Get me out of here," I responded. "I want to be traded. I want to get out of Florida."

"Okay," he said. "It's your call. You know the trading deadline is passed, we will wait until the off-season."

"This place has become a nightmare," I ranted on. "I came here with promise of big money and continued exposure. I find a very beautiful girl, who turns out to be nothing but a figment of my imagination, and suddenly, I am left jumping at the air and making a total fool of myself. I don't have any more friends, and everyone has shut me outside and left me hanging to dry." I took another swig from my bottle and then tossed it away.

"Well," Fred relied. "I tried to warn you about your choices, and you went on to pursue them nonetheless. How does it feel?"

"I don't want to talk about it," I said. "I just want out of town."

I staggered up the stairs, my head woozy from the alcohol. Stumbling into my room, I stared up at her pictures once again.

"Cherrie," I called aloud. "Cherrie, come down from the wall and be mine. Come back to me." With that, I drifted off to sleep.

Chapter 8

EARLY THE FOLLOWING morning, I took to the court out in the park nearby. Still under much emotional stress, I felt I needed a change in scenery, and perhaps some company with the public. I knew I would not be alone for long, when others would come around to use the space.

Indeed, a handful of guys came along, asking for autographs. A few of them began calling and texting their friends to come over to where we were. A few began asking me about my slumping game.

I was moved inside. "I'm sorry," I responded. "But I just... I don't know. This place holds too many nightmares. Perhaps it is time to move somewhere else."

"Mr. Molokai Express, you're not leaving, are you?" one young boy asked, shocked at my suggestion. "You can't leave us."

"Well can you not get someone else who won't fall all over himself on the court?" I said, lightening up a little. "A trade won't hurt."

Beginning to feel normal again, I took the ball, and once again I was demonstrating my signature dribbles and shots. After a while, I rounded some of the guys up and we began to play a round of basketball.

It wasn't long before a newspaper reporter showed up at the park, covering the unfolding game and interviewing some of the fans present. He got several pictures in the process as we continued playing. When I caught the news the next day, I saw the headlines, "Heat Superstar Involved in Community Activities." I laughed when I saw papers, which seemed to suggest I was involved in a charitable event.

The nightmare finally came to an end just days later while in Washington, DC. As I was getting ready to leave my hotel room, I answered a knock at the door.

There stood Cherrie, ring on her finger. "I finally put it on," she said. "I do."

Overwhelmed with relief, I pulled her close and kissed her. Once illusive as a gazelle, she was now a dream come true. Here we stood, armed locked around each other.

Having regained my form, I returned to my normal self and we sailed through the season, ultimately winning the NBA title that summer.

We were married three months later in Puerto Rico, where Mr. Hoover had a villa. Our festivities were much smaller, given her desire to keep a low profile. Only our close friends and family were present.

I was a little bit annoyed by her paranoia, but suddenly I realized there was a price tag to marrying this girl. I was not used to the absence of the flash of cameras and the bustle of the press, and in a way, looked forward to extensive coverage during the wedding, but she refused to get married with the press about.

There were about a hundred people present, not including the attendants. My brother Fred served as best man, and Mr. Hoover, as her stepfather was giving Cherrie away.

I was teary eyed for the first time in a long time when she came walking down the short aisle leading to the altar, set on a large patio opening out to the beach. As she arrived, an appointed judge sat everyone down and proceeded with the ceremony.

I could not take my eyes off of the girl, garbed in that frilly white gown. She had never looked more beautiful than before. The ceremony dragged on, until we got to the instrumental line.

"I now pronounce you husband and wife, you may now kiss the bride."

I swept her into my arms and we kissed to the applause of the rest of the crowd. She was mine, and my goal had been reached.

That night, however, she somehow disappeared, shortly after the reception. I had unsuccessfully tried to track her down, but when I could not find her, I reported her missing to the Florida authorities.

A month later, shortly after our season opener in Chicago, I had received a tip from one of our friends that she was getting married again, to another man, Mr. Ted Lincoln from Detroit. But shortly after her wedding ceremony, she had been arrested by the deputies. On hearing that news, I hopped in my car and sped off to Detroit.

I was greatly disturbed inside, to see her vanish with the wind like this; for she had gone and backstabbed me before I could even have a fair chance to really be with her, as I had with other girls I had gone with. My highest dreams would remain elusive and nothing could fill that gap.

Interlogue

MURMURS RIPPLED THROUGH the crowd as Harry finished his story and then pulled out his marriage license. It was signed, sealed, and committed, and she was indeed guilty of violating it by going to the altar with another man. The cameras flashed ever more rapidly as he came down from the stand. Reporters were eagerly waiting to hear the other side of the story, expecting to uncover a juicy conspiracy.

"Will the defense present their testimony?" the judge asked.

"Your Honour, I would like to call upon Mr. Theodore Lincoln," requested the defense lawyer. It was a surprising move to some that he called upon the "star witness" instead of the defendant, but brushing off the surprise, they leaned in once again to listen to the other side of the story.

Theodore Lincoln, a Ford Motor Company heir, was once a platoon commander within the Navy SEAL's highly secretive DEVGRU division. He had participated in numerous missions around the globe, and was believed to be involved in the capture of numerous high-profile terrorists. Since his operations were secret, however, nobody was able to verify if it were so.

The man solemnly stood and made his way to the stand. He was slightly older than Harry, a tick shorter, but more heavily built, with broader shoulders and a larger chest. He was clean-shaven with black hair and grey eyes. He carried himself with an air or authority and dignity with none of the first man's cockiness.

"Do you swear to tell the truth, the whole truth, and nothing but the truth?" asked the bailiff.

"I do."

"Mr. Lincoln," began the defending attorney, "please tell us about your involvement with the defendant."

Ted's story: Chapter 1

LOVE IS A FORCE OF nature, stronger than the mightiest of men. It brings people together and gives them hope and a purpose for living and doing what they do. But it can also destroy and kill. That is why it must be harnessed and controlled, and the object of your love must be someone who will never leave you or let you down. I would learn this lesson the hard way, when my own life had taken a hit because of love.

Cherrie's mother, Marie, had worked in a clothing factory in North Carolina, where she also had a relationship with a NASCAR driver. That ended when he refused to father the child when she was born. At the same time, the factory where she had worked had closed down. That led her to relocate to Dearborn, Michigan, where she had found work in our Ford assembly line.

My folks, who ran the company since then, were aware that she could not afford housing of her own, and so they took her into our home. They had stayed with us for five years until she had saved enough money to move into a rented apartment, not too far from the assembly line.

Since she was busy putting long hours at work, my twin sister Tammy and I were often put in charge of taking care of her daughter ever since she was an infant. That would continue even after they had moved out of our house. We greatly delighted being with this charming and playful little girl, who had become like a little sister to us. We would pick her up from the daycare on her way home from school and would continue to take care of her, taking turns playing with her while the other did homework. As she grew older, we would walk her to and from school early in the morning, and she would stay at our house until her mother came home from work. The three of us would become the best of friends.

Marie was an ambitious woman. She was determined to make it on her own and become a fashion designer, running her own line of designer clothing. After work, she would take evening classes in a fashion school here in Michigan. She had spent much of her precious spare time sewing, knitting, and designing clothes. She often saved up her income to obtain better fabrics and before long, she was fashioning with silk.

She had also put Cherrie into modelling. Since infancy, her pictures had often fetched "cutest baby" awards, and her mother realized she had potential as a model. From age three, she began participating in junior pageants, ultimately participating in the International Junior Miss. She would appear onstage modelling any one of her mother's formal evening wear and informal wear, and as part of the "optional" criteria, she would do a ballet dance or play a piano piece.

Cherrie herself loved modelling. She loved fashions. And she loved to perform her spiel. Every time she came onstage dressed in her wear, she carried herself with the natural charm and grace that stole the hearts of the judges and audiences. And she was also a talented dancer and pianist. Her accomplishments fetched high acclaim, annually landing her in the top five finalists in her respective age group.

The other girls in school soon became jealous of her beauty and fame. They began to shun her, and soon influenced other boys to do the same, until Cherrie had no other friends. Before long, others began to tease her and call her names. In their eyes, they tore her down into a "wannabe Miss World," and began to feel special when shunning her.

At first, Cherrie was not discouraged to want to opt out of junior pageant. She relished getting up to present her ware to the crowd, exuding natural charm and charisma in her presentations. We continued to support her and encouraged her to keep going.

"It's part of the responsibility of being you," Tammy had once told her. "Girls get jealous when someone so famous comes along."

Before long, however, Cherrie was beginning to feel insecure, even terrified. I felt that she wanted to stop doing pageants, but did not have the courage to tell anyone about it. Tammy and I were her only friends, but by now, we were in high school and could no longer be there with her. The other kids continued to bully her, throwing stuff at her, punching her, and one time, even locking her in a broom closet.

Of course we wasted no time complaining to our parents whenever she came home with a bruised face. Once she disclosed who her bullies were, they in turn reported these mistreatments to the school officials. Numerous kids were suspended or detained for their bullying tactics. Unfortunately, this did not seem to deter them. Suspended kids became hardened and more relentless with their bullying upon reinstatement.

I was not going to stand for such viciousness anymore. I really hated what they were doing to Cherrie, making her feel belittled and vulnerable, just because they themselves were losers who were jealous of her fame. One of these days, I was going to put them in their place.

One day, during lunchtime between classes, Tammy and I were having our lunch just outside the school when we saw Cherrie come running toward us from the elementary school just a block away. She had a blackened eye, above her bleeding nose. I was stunned to see her here.

"Cherrie!" I gasped. "What on earth happened, little girl?"

"Oh, Teddy, Tammy, some boy just whacked me in the face just now during recess!" she cried. "They threatened to deface me, one eye at a time! And so I ran away from them to come find you guys."

Tammy took her into her arms. "Cherrie, Cherrie," she said reassuringly, "It's okay. I'm here for you."

"Don't let those kids get to you," I snapped angrily. "They're just a bunch of losers."

"Yeah, well I wish I could get out, and go somewhere else," she sobbed. "Oh, my life is becoming a living hell now. Everyone is just making life miserable, just because I'm not like everyone else."

"Again, they're just a bunch of losers," I responded. "I am going to show them up for the losers they are."

"Tearing them down to size, that's not going to help," Tammy interjected. "Can't you see she needs to be comforted?"

"Yes, I'm sorry. I'm just getting really angry now."

Just then, a burst of laughter erupted behind us. I turned and saw a pack of kids pointing us out and laughing.

"Oh, there she is, America's dolly," one boy mocked, pointing her out. "Hanging onto each other like..."

That was when something snapped in me. I got up, grabbed him by the shoulders, and slammed him into the wall.

"You little coward," I responded. "You don't have the guts to say that you're all jealous of Cherrie."

"You big bully!" he exploded. "How dare you..."

"You get a life, you loser. If you ever touch her again, you will have me to answer to." I glared at the other kids. "And that goes for all of you too. If you can't stand in the presence of such greatness, you feel compelled to rip her down to size. Well, you all will never amount to anything, so get a life and put your energy to good use." I could still feel my face glowering even as the kids turned and walked away, visibly intimidated.

I have never bullied anyone in school, and normally wouldn't have physically manhandled a kid half my size. But I knew I had to protect Cherrie, and when everything else fails, put them in their place.

Cherrie was amazed as they left. "Wow Teddy, you really stood up to those guys," she was saying.

"That's how you put them in their place," Tammy added. "They didn't dare to fight back again."

"I had to do something," I answered. "I cannot put up with this anymore. Now, I don't expect any more trouble."

"I hope so," both girls said, and we walked her back to the school, informing the principal about what had happened.

Following the encounter, fewer of the kids dared to pick on Cherrie. Before long, they began to allow her into their social circles. And when she gratefully accepted their company without any fear of bullying or conceitedness of her fame, they no longer felt jealous or intimidated by her. She fit in with the crowd and exuding her playful and energetic side, became the life of the party and due to her fame, gave her whole group of friends a sense of prestige.

Unfortunately, some of the kids began to sense that she was still somewhat naïve and thus easy to manipulate. They gradually began to exploit this weakness by enticing her to spend more time with "the cooler crowd." Of course, since Tammy and I had homework to focus on and had little spare time, Cherrie began to spend more time hanging out with these other kids rather than with us.

We began to notice changes when Cherrie no longer came home with us after school. Instead, she began to spend more time with her friends at their homes, often having sleepovers. Tammy and I were happy to see Cherrie making friends and having fun, but naturally we still missed her and felt somewhat betrayed, since we had to help her make friends.

I remember clearly that afternoon when I caught Cherrie after school while she was waiting for her friends. It was coming to the end of the year and we were preparing for examinations. Tammy and I were wrapping up ninth grade, our final year before high school. Cherrie was coming to the end of third grade.

"Cherrie," I called, "hey Cherrie, little girl."

She just looked in my direction. "Stop calling me 'little girl,'" she said, "I'm no little girl anymore."

"Okay, then big girl," I replied, "where are you off to now?"

"I'm going to meet up with some of my friends. We've got this end-of-year school play we're working on. We're going to hold a slumber party afterward."

"Oh, good work," I said. "You did very well in last year's performance."

"What are you up to?"

"I just wanted to check up on my little sister. I've been missing her."

Cherrie blushed. "I'm sorry. I guess I have been caught up with stuff."

"And you forgot that you owe your friends to your big brother and sister." I gently put my arm around her. "These same friends of yours, once upon a time, had been your worst tormentors."

Just then, her friends called to her. "Sorry," she said, "I have to go." And she was off again. I sighed to myself briefly, and then shrugged. I don't own this girl forever.

Our worst nightmares came true the following day in school. That morning, I had a gut feeling that Cherrie had been in some sort of trouble, but I could not be sure, for I was in class and she was away in the elementary school. Or was she?

At lunch time, I quickly ran over to the elementary school to check on her. I found her friend Molly, with whom she had been staying. She was looking bewildered, and scared beyond her wits.

"We were running overtime for rehearsals," she whispered. "We stayed later than we should have. I don't even remember going home. Last I recall I fell asleep after rehearsals ran late. Next thing I know, I wake up in my own bed, with all my friends there. Except for Cherrie.

"My parents did ask me if I'd been drinking," she continued. "They said that my eyes looked bloodshot."

"How did you get home?" I asked.

"Mr. Jackson, our drama teacher, dropped us off," she replied, "and explained to my folks that we had fallen asleep. He was kind enough to explain that we had to run overtime. And he did provide us with stuff to eat."

Immediately, I had a gut feeling that something was amiss. I rushed off to find Mr. Jackson, who I eventually found in his office.

"Hi Ted," he greeted me, looking up from behind his desk. "What can I do for you?"

"I was looking for Cherrie," I answered. "Molly said that everyone fell asleep on you while practicing last night."

"That they did," he responded. "Well, only Cherrie, Molly, and three of their friends fell asleep. As I prepared to drop them off, Cherrie began to vomit up. I took her temperature and she was developing a fever. So I rushed her to the hospital." He sighed and added, "I feel bad. I pushed these kids too hard and it was terribly irresponsible to keep them up so late, past their bed time. But we have too much work to do, with performances coming up tomorrow. And now Cherrie is in the hospital. I just called her mother this morning."

"Thank you," I said, and turned to leave. But something about him made me feel uncomfortable.

When I got back to school, I found Tammy in the cafeteria and right away and beckoned her over to a solitary table, where we could talk in peace.

"Tammy," I began, "Mr. Jackson had said that he had rushed Cherrie to the hospital because she had some food poisoning, but I have a feeling that maybe something is still amiss."

"I don't know," she replied, "but I have a feeling that he is not on the up-and-up."

"You mean..."

"I talked to another of her friends, who talked about having fallen asleep in the theatre and waking up in Molly's house, remembering nothing about coming home. Her parents described her them as having bloodshot eyes, as though they were drinking."

"That's right, and Molly concurred that."

"Do you think that he had drugged them?"

"That's possible." I could no longer eat. I stood up and immediately made my way to the front office, asking for the number to the hospital.

That afternoon was rode with great tension on our minds, as our parents picked us up early and we rushed to the hospital to check up on Cherrie. We learned how the doctors, initially believing she had food poisoning as Mr. Jackson had reported, in actuality, discovered that she needed treatment for drug overdose. They described how she not only had been vomiting and had a high fever, but she was behaving out of control and her mental makeup had become suspect. They had to get a psychiatrist to try and figure out what was wrong with her, but she would not talk, but only throw a fuss.

Unfortunately, we realized that there was even more to the story. As we went in to see Cherrie, she leapt out of the bed at us, whimpering and crying out. We quickly gathered around her and held her close.

"Oh, oh, oh," she squeaked.

Cherrie, who had not spoken at all, according to the doctors, proceeded to tell us the whole story. He had drugged her and all her friends that previous evening, so she fell asleep before rehearsals were over. The next thing she realized, rather than dropping her off at Molly's with the rest of her friends, he had taken her into his home and proceeded to sexually molest her. Cherrie was so tormented by that experience that her blood began to boil with fear and she began to kick and scream. She soon began to throw up from hyperventilation, and Mr. Jackson, took her to the hospital, conveniently explaining these "symptoms" as food poisoning.

Word of this scandal soon swept through the national media by the end of the day. Mr. Jackson had been swiftly arrested, amidst a swarm of angry parents and cowering children. Our phone had been ringing off the hook with calls from several news reporters, as well as everyone we knew.

Cherrie had been called to appear on several different news programs and talk shows. Her story was constantly met with mounting outrage nationwide against child abduction and molestation. So great had the anti-pedophile sentiment had grown, that rates of abduction had actually fallen. Several attempted abductions had been met with violent lynching from surrounding witnesses.

Inside, Cherrie was so deeply devastated by her experience, that after several weeks of counsel and psychiatry, we realized it would be best for her and her mother to relocate, ultimately to Miami, Florida, where my family owned a vacation home. By now, her mother, having garnered sufficient experience with designing and making clothes, felt it was time to launch out on her own and begin her fashion business. My folks offered to help provide her with the necessary initial capital and allowed her to live in the vacation home until they could buy their own place.

Chapter 2

THESE CHILDHOOD EVENTS had done Cherrie much mental and emotional damage at such a critical moment in her life. Having no real father was especially difficult, for she had nobody who could support her and strengthen her.

Nonetheless, she continued her career as a model, signing on with an agency down in Florida at age 12, and began representing several fashion houses, including one her mother had just launched. She continued to appear in beauty pageants, winning more national and international titles, and ultimately, she won the Miss Universe title in her first year of eligibility.

As she grew in fame, Marie's business steadily grew, eventually exploding after her daughter won her first Miss United States title, and booming further with every succeeding title she had won. They soon generated a nine-figure income and expanded their business well beyond Florida.

Cherrie was commonly regarded as the world's most beautiful woman, a perception solidified after People's Magazine had named her the Eighth Wonder when she won her first Miss Universe title. This new nickname had stuck with her; she was a full-fledged celebrity, modelling for twelve different fashion houses, in the States and abroad.

But it didn't stop there; she appeared in advertisements for vacation spots, sporting events, even car commercials. She appeared in several television shows, and twice appeared in a ballet. She also served as a cheerleader for the Miami Heat.

Outside of the spotlight, she had gone to a fashion school herself down in Florida, intending to become a designer herself. She had often joined her mother in the studio, picking out fabrics, sketching, sewing, and weaving, and she had a natural eye for design. And in her spare time, she enjoyed tinkering away at the piano or spending time behind the wheel of either one of her favourite toys, her 1967 Ace Shelby Cobra or her airboat.

Yes she was a full-blown celebrity, living a life most girls could only dream of. And while she had fun participating in many of these things, at the end of the day, it only drained her emotionally when nobody gave her the real love she needed. Sure, there were a lot of guys who were clamouring to date her, and she often accepted their attention, but after going with someone on just one date, she would feel uncomfortable with them and no longer go with them.

What she really needed was someone who truly loved her, but I scarcely thought I would eventually be the one. I loved her as a sister, but I never had any real romantic intentions.

Meanwhile, after I had graduated from high school, I had followed in my father's footsteps and enrolled in naval academy. After three years of intensive training, I eventually enlisted with the Navy SEALs. I had served on Team Four for two years, before eventually being moved to DEVGRU. After serving three years as an operator, I was eventually promoted to platoon commander.

To my father and me, military service is a sign of patriotism, a love for country. We live in a nation that had been born when our fathers gave their lives, and ensuring its survival meant ongoing battles against forces determined to tear us apart. The Lincoln family had a long history of militia service, dating back to the War of Independence. My father had fought in the Vietnam War and had been on mission in several other operations before returning to Michigan. His father had been a World War II veteran. I was to carry on the tradition.

Every year, I would be given a one week leave, during which time, I would normally go home to my family in Michigan. But this one year, I happened to have been given leave over Cherrie's 21st birthday, and so I flew down to Florida where the rest of my family would join us.

Upon arriving at our vacation house, after having set down my luggage and taken a shower, I called her up.

"Ted, you're in Florida??" her anxious voice sounded on the other end.

"I'm here," I replied. "Family should be arriving by tomorrow, but I'm..." Suddenly the phone was cut off.

Within ten minutes, a screeching of tires could be heard, as she had arrived. By the time I had come out to greet her, an excited Cherrie came bounding out of her Cobra. She quickly grabbed my hand, tugging me to come with her. "I really got to talk to you," she said. "Hop in, we got to go someplace."

Even into her twenties, she still carries a child-like air. She'd sooner drag me down to the playground and beg me to push her on the swings or go play hide and seek. Right now, she was dragging me into her car to go someplace. And before long, the thunderous roar could be heard as she unleashed 500 horsepower driving through Miami Beach, before turning and flying down Highway 1 extending out to the Florida Keys.

"We're going to one of my favourite places," she was saying.

"Cherrie, you've got such a lead foot there," I gasped, looking at the speedometer. "Take it easy."

"And wait until sunset?" she whined. "We've got to get away."

I knew that by the way she was desperate that she wanted to talk to me alone.

"I want us to wait until we get to where we're going," she was saying. "I can't talk until we get there."

We drove on until we came to Largo Sound. She wheeled her car into a parking spot and cut the motor. Reaching over into the glove compartment, she pulled out a package of earplugs.

"You'll want these," she said. "We're going for a noisy boat ride."

"I'm guessing we're going for a trip into the Everglades."

"That's right," she replied. "We're going to take the airboat. I got to learn how to drive the thing over last spring."

We hopped out of the car and approached an airboat docked near the end of the dock. As we boarded, I helped her untie the boat, before pushing off into the water. We began inserting our earplugs, before Cherrie climbed into the driver's seat in the rear, and began tying her hair into a bun.

The engine started with a roar, followed by the rushing spray from the propellers behind her. Cherrie stepped on it, and soon, we were flying north-west across the stretch of sea, toward the Florida Everglades which took up most of the southern portion of the state. Meanwhile, I sat back, enjoying the rush of wind blowing on us and watching the miles of ocean scenery going by.

We sailed onwards until we began entering the marshy wetlands. Cherrie slowed down dramatically to maneuver through the region and avoid letting anything get caught in the propellers.

I crinkled my nose at the smell of the wetlands, somewhat surprised that she would particularly enjoy coming out here. Cherrie certainly had an unusual sense of adventure at times. Still, I loved to explore and waited patiently to see what she wanted to come and see me about.

We sailed through the wetlands, driving over the tall grass through some boggy soil, as was possible in an airboat. Eventually, we came upon a pasture-like region surrounded by tall grass. In the distance, I saw a solitary tree. Out here, it was not so smelly as some of the wetlands we had passed through earlier.

Cherrie maneuvered the boat to a stop and then cut the engine. Removing her earplugs, she climbed out of the rear driver's seat to the bench next to me.

"Okay, we're alone," I began. "What did you want to talk about?"

Cherrie sighed. "Well, I have been coming to the end of my rope," she said. "I have told you in my letters all about what I had been going through, how the public keeps digging into my private life and with so many guys pursuing me. I have been on the verge of a nervous breakdown."

Saying nothing, I just looked her in the eye with a slight nod, and then gently took her hand reassuringly.

"I love fashions and modelling them, but when they put so much pressure on me while under the spotlight, it is no longer fun." She sighed and added, "This American Dream, when I first got my taste of it, was sweet, but it soon turned bitter. I have a nice life and all, but by now it is really wearing me down."

I was moved deeply inside. Until now, I had only imagined what she was going through, but now, my thoughts were verified. When her father had left, her mother had gone and sold themselves to the American Dream, hoping for a better life, but that instead became a poison to her soul.

I reached out and pulled her close beside me. "I'm always here for you," I said. "And now I'm more frustrated than before that your father had abandoned you."

She smiled and a tear formed in her eye. "Thank you," she said. "I know you mean it, not like the line of men who merely say they do, but they don't really."

I grimaced at her graphic description, but she said it. Somehow, I wished I could be there for her. But this was when the first seeds have been planted.

We spent about an hour in the bayou talking more about the matter before we decided to return to Miami. Cherrie climbed back into the high seat and proceeded to crank up the engine.

The engine sounded somewhat muffled as it started up. She revved the motor, before putting it into gear. She turned the boat around and proceeded back the way we came. We were probably about halfway back to the ocean when the engine gave out.

Cherrie pumped on the throttle and tried to start the engine. It cranked and cranked but it would not turn over. "Oh, no," she moaned. "I think I'm out of fuel. How silly of me not to fill up. Guess we have to call for help." As she pulled out her mobile phone, she gasped again. "Oh, no, no," she moaned again. "No service."

Meanwhile, I had pulled out my own phone. No good, I was also zero bars. "Mine too," I said. "It looks like we're stranded out here. Have you no radio beacon or something?"

"I could try that," she responded, switching on the device. "The homing device should work."

Ten minutes went by. As we sat and waited, I perked my ear at a sound in the distance. Was that thunder? Looking up at the skies, the clouds were gathering and growing dark and stormy.

"Looks like we've got a bigger problem at hand," I said. "It looks like we're going to have a little weather coming."

"I didn't even bring a raincoat," Cherrie complained. "We were supposed to have bright and sunny weather over the whole week."

The sounds of thunder grew closer and rain began to fall. Cherrie climbed in next to me, and we huddled close together as the lightning lit the sky.

I looked up at the homing beacon again. Surely, the coast guard should pick up the signal, but could they find us in the downpour?

When I looked back at Cherrie, her eyes were almost alive with adventure.

"You've picked quite the meeting place," I whispered, "the rainy wetlands in the middle of nowhere."

At that, she began to giggle. "Oh," she gasped, "here we are stuck in the middle of slimy, smelly swampland, in a thunderstorm, and completely out of contact with anyone by phone and having nowhere to go, except to wait and see if the coast guard can pick us up." She sighed and added, "At least you're here protecting me and watching over me. I don't know what I'd do."

I kissed her forehead and sat back as the downpour continued to drench us. There was no point in trying to stay dry now, but we still lay low to avoid the lightning.

I did not keep track of how long the downpour lasted. I continued to look upward, hoping a rescue crew could somehow spot us. The coast guard could pick up our coordinates, but it was too dark and misty to see anything by helicopter. It was too difficult to navigate the swamp by boat. I held on and said a silent prayer, hoping for a miracle.

Before long, we began to hear a boat navigating through the water. I saw a hovercraft coming in toward where we were. I stood and waved my arms, and was met with a beam of light as they saw us.

"Just in the nick of time," I shouted out to a crew member as he stepped out to the deck.

"We caught your signal," he replied. "It was difficult to navigate through the swamplands. We had been going in circles for some time."

He tossed us a rope, and began pulling us in once I had tied down our boat. "We'll tow you on back to the moorage," he called out. "You come on into the cabin."

Cherrie was laughing as I led her up onto the deck of the hovercraft and into the cabin. Her hair and clothes were all drenched and unkempt, but she seemed not to care. She was visually relieved to be rescued.

"Oh, now this is an adventure I'll remember for years to come," she had been saying.

"Just imagine if you had to appear on the catwalk, looking like this," I teased her.

"I couldn't care less. I'm having the time of my life."

Inside the cabin, there were four rescue workers, who began tending to us, fetching towels and checking our body temperature.

Cherrie's birthday was three days later. Looking for ideas for a party to throw her, I talked to her best friend in town, fellow model and cheerleader Julie Garfield. We discussed some of Cherrie's concerns that she had expressed to me while out on the marsh.

"I think Cherrie is for one part, feeling under-appreciated as a person," she had been saying. "She feels she is like a public figure, adored by many, but not appreciated like a person."

"How many real friends does she have around here?"

"Oh, there's only like three other girls whom we hang out with. A few other acquaintances here and there. After that, just a bunch of business colleagues."

"I see," I replied. "So what kind of things do you do in down time?"

"We rarely get downtime, but we mostly hang out at the beach," she said. "If we do something for her birthday, we should somehow make it a special occasion. I could try and negotiate for more time off."

"Okay," I responded. "I do have until the end of the week before I have to leave."

At her suggestion, we decided we would gather some of our friends and take her up to Disney World in Orlando. We wound up inviting just over twenty people, her closest friends in Florida, along with a few others from back home. Each of the guests would pay their way at Disney World, plus some extra for Cherrie's own fare and would contribute presents. It would be our own little special time.

Having our plan set in place, we sent everyone ahead of us to Orlando, while we proceeded to "kidnap" Cherrie. The day before her birthday, instead of coming home from work, her mother would drive her to Ft. Lauderdale for dinner. My family would join them out there, but once we got into the car, instead of going back to

Miami, we would be going toward Orlando, where everyone was waiting for her.

The two girls arrived at the Ft. Lauderdale restaurant on schedule, as the sun was setting. After dinner, we got into our Lincoln Navigator and drove off northbound.

Cherrie was so tired after a long day's work that she quickly lay down to sleep in the back bench. "Wake me up when we get home," she had said.

How convenient. She would not know where we were going and we would be able to keep everything a surprise.

It was a long, uneventful trip as we made our way north. Before long, the rest of the women were fast asleep. Several times, I had gazed back at Cherrie sleeping soundly on her mother's lap. Marie was also sound asleep, as was Tammy next to me, and my mother in the front seat. But I was too excited for the plans laid ahead, that I could not sleep.

We were halfway toward Orlando when, my father pulled over and asked me to take over driving, so he could get rest. Since I still had stamina, I gladly obliged and made it the rest of the way to Orlando.

Cherrie was awake by the time we made it to Disney World. Looking around, she seemed somewhat stunned by all the bright lights. "Where are we?" she asked with a start.

"You'll see," I heard her mother whisper.

Meanwhile, I had pulled the vehicle up to the main entrance of Disney World, where our crowd had been waiting for us. They began to cheer as we pulled up.

I shut down the engine and bounded out to open the rear passenger door. Tammy came out first, followed by Marie, who stood by the door. As Cherrie eased her way out, the crowd surrounding us erupted into a cheer.

"SURPRISE!!!"

"What on earth?" Cherrie gasped.

"Happy birthday little girl and welcome to Disney World," Tammy responded, as Cherrie gazed on at everyone present.

Julie did not hesitate bounding out of the mass of crowd to give her a hug. "Happy 21st birthday girl!" she said. "Welcome to official adulthood."

At first, Cherrie peeled back, until she looked into the crowd and recognized the faces of several of her friends. She realized this was mostly family and friends in the crowd.

I took her aside briefly. "This is your last chance at being a child," I had whispered, and she giggled. She then slowly began to realize that she had more true friends than she realized.

The following morning was packed with activity as our group made our way through the various activities and attractions at Disney World. Throughout the day, Tammy and I had accompanied Cherrie, along with some of her closer friends. Once again, she was becoming a little child. She greeted all the different animated characters before her, often laughing and smiling at them. Whenever we rode a roller coaster, she'd grip my hand before we'd plunge down a sharp drop.

Of course, there were other guests who recognized Cherrie and were constantly coming up to her, taking her picture and asking for autographs. It wasn't long before the press came swarming into Disney World to get pictures and sound bites from her. But as I observed her, she seemed not to care today because she was touched to know that she had truly been loved.

While swimming at the waterpark, as we climbed in from the pool onto a floating Mickey Mouse boat, Cherrie leaned over and thanked me again for such a wonderful surprise.

"I never knew how many people really appreciated me," she was saying.

I smiled back at her. "I thought bringing you out here with all your friends would be a great birthday present," I replied. "I know it seems like so many guys are just out to use you for your beauty and fame, but there still are others who truly care about you."

"Thank you again. You can never know how lonely it feels to be just another product on the shelf, but to have no real friends."

"That's a sad life. You know, now I almost wish that our folks could have foreseen this path. This so called American Dream really is no easy street. The glamour, glitz, and fame, it really is a cost to the soul. Your life is no longer your own."

"I couldn't have said that better."

"But at least you still have some true friends. They still love you for you, not because you're just someone to wow them. I'd like to see how many of those Heats stars have this many true friends."

"Yeah, Well, I don't really know anything about those guys. To be honest, I keep away from them, because they're determined to make their bed with me in it."

"That's because they are just a bunch of shallow souls."

"Yes. And the press wants to glamorize it all. I'm on magazine covers with many of those players. I appear with some in television shows and commercials. They try and speculate who gets to sleep with me, and at times, they try and set me up, but I never give in."

"I admire you for keeping your purity," I said. "It's not easy for any young woman in your shoes."

We were suddenly interrupted by someone whistling at her and waving. I chuckled lightly.

"Here we go again," I added. "Besides, don't you feel lucky to be this beautiful?"

"When I was young, that's all that mattered to me," she answered. "But if I weren't so beautiful as a child, I would never have expected to have my identity wrapped in my beauty and all. That wonderful blessing has become a bitter curse."

"That's sad. But again, don't let anyone define you by your beauty alone."

By the end of the day, we had gathered in the ballroom, which we had booked out for a formal banquet. We chose to do a Cinderella theme, with Cherrie as Cinderella. I was the Prince. And just for the heck of it, Julie and Tammy opted to be the stepsisters, while my mother and her mother, becoming children once more, posed as the stepmother and godmother respectively. Of course they clawed at her from time to time that evening, and Cherrie played along and bickered back playfully.

Following the meal, we danced away. By my own admission, I was a little awkward at first, having never danced in years, but with Cherrie as an expert, I soon caught on as we took to the floor, gliding across the room, and before long, everyone else joined in. But when the clock struck twelve, even though we didn't script it, Cherrie bolted out of the room, kicking off her shoe.

Playing along, I picked up the shoe, and had Julie and Tammy try it on. Ironically, the shoe did fit them, but following convention, they pretended it didn't.

"Well I guess I will have to keep searching," I concluded. "I shall not rest until I find her." We all laughed as we made our way back to bed.

We spent three more days in Disney World. During that time, Cherrie was much more relaxed, and not so fearful in public. She was opening up, not only to our other friends, but even strangers, and I saw her greeting others in the park, giving out autographs, and posing for pictures with other young girls.

"I wish I could be you," I once heard someone say.

Cherrie responded with a laugh. "I'm just a clothing saleswoman."

I jabbed at her. "There's someone who doesn't really know what it's really like to live the American Dream."

It was a fun four days at Disney World. For a time, a few of us had stepped back into childhood, to celebrate her 21 years, and she enjoyed every moment of it, for once not feeling so much under pressure. After the four days came to an end and we returned back to Miami, I agreed to keep in touch with her regularly.

Chapter 3

MY PLATOON WAS DEPLOYED to overseas the following week. We were stationed at an undisclosed location overseas where our Staff Headquarters had deemed it necessary to keep a DEVGRU platoon stationed on the base, in the event of a major strike.

There had been plenty of terrorist activity in this region. Government officials and innocent civilians had been taken hostage. Random bombings occurred. So far, we were able to thwart their efforts, but we knew the enemy was relentless. They would strike back.

I had lost so many allies in battle. A helicopter had been gunned down. An overland convoy had hit a roadside bomb, killing half of the men. I knew many of the soldiers who had died; I had two cousins and many others had been my close friends. Knowing the dangerous nature of this mission made me all the more wary of the dangers of our operation and that I was a brush away from death myself.

Every morning, I would gather the men early to conduct roll call. We would embark on our practice drills and conditioning tests until ten in the morning. At which time, I would convene with our Troop HQ for two hours. We would adjourn for lunch before continuing with combat training outside of the base. Everyone would report back to the base by six for dinner, and lights are out by eight thirty sharp. Sundays were different, at ten we would assemble for a church service conducted by the chaplain on base, praying and going over Scripture.

I had been to church as a child years ago. Our entire family had made profession to be saved, and had made regular practice of doing good, which was the main reason why we took Marie and Cherrie into our home. As time went on, however, we had little time for God or Scriptures. But now, something about these messages had caught my attention, but I could not be sure what to make of it. I thought I was doing fine, but somehow deep inside, I felt something was missing.

The whole time I was there, I made sure to write letters every evening just ten minutes before lights out. I wrote to my parents every Monday and to Tammy every Wednesday. I wrote to Cherrie on Thursday and her mother on Saturday. I talked to them about my daily routine, giving them small highlights on our progress and briefed them on the unfolding mission as it happened. And I heard back from them regularly, most often from Cherrie.

We had been there for about four months when in a dream one evening, I was assigned to rescue hostages. I remember bursting into a secret cave in the mountains. After moving through the corridor, I proceeded to search the caves for prisoners. When I burst into one room, I found Cherrie all tied up and gagged. I untied her and took the gag out of her mouth.

"Ted!" she exclaimed. "Just in the..."

I put my hand to my mouth, telling her to keep quiet, and we quietly stepped out of the room and moved through the corridor back to the entrance. We were soon ambushed by her kidnappers, all fully armed. They demanded that I put down my weapons, telling us that we were both to be held hostage.

I complied, setting down my weapon, before suddenly striking one of the kidnappers with a quick blow to the jaw. Before anyone else could react, I had knocked out two more opponents and now held two guns in my hands. I shot two men who attempted to grab Cherrie, and then quickly attacked another one.

The rest of the men fled and Cherrie, relieved that I'd saved her, threw her arms around me.

"First it's my career, then men stalking me, now terrorists," she said. "You've saved me from them all."

As we made our way out of there, she proceeded to tell me her story. She had been in Tel-Aviv, Israel for a fashion show, when spies captured her. She talked about having been mugged while walking down the street. The next thing she realized, she was tied up and gagged by the enemy, who told them they were holding her hostage for a new ultimatum: the withdrawal of American forces by that weekend or they put her to death.

"Threatening them with the death of the Eighth Wonder of the World would certainly force the Americans' hand," she had recalled her captor's words. "Imagine the uproar from their public if she dies because they don't withdraw."

I turned and hugged her, promising not to let anything happen to her. "You're safe with me," I said. "You can stay by my side while I'm on duty."

As we spoke, other SEALs came to our aid. Storming the cave, they found her captors and had them incarcerated. Other fugitives were released. We accompanied them all back to the base, where they would soon be flown home.

When we arrived back in the base, Cherrie and I had been given some time to ourselves and we went for a walk in a park somewhere outside the city.

As we were going down a quiet path, she turned and tugged at my arm. "Ted, you're like a guardian angel to me," she had said. "One moment, I was in Israel, doing a show, the next thing I know, I'm captured and held hostage by the enemy, and they're sure to put me to death. And then who should come to my rescue but you? I had no idea you were coming to rescue me."

I smiled at her, and then took her under my arm as she went on.

"Ted, will you continue to hold me through the storm? Will you be there?"

The rest of that day, she stayed by my side, as I was stationed on the Tigris docks at Baghdad, Iraq to inspect incoming cargo and by night, she accompanied me as I made my nightly rounds to enforce a curfew throughout the city.

The following morning, we were stationed at the port again when air raid sirens suddenly went off. Hostile aircraft flew overhead unexpectedly, firing at us. Our forces began firing back at them, but a missile landed near us. The subsequent explosion blew us back many yards, destroying the docks and killing many of the workers there. Gunfire and explosions rained down.

Cherrie and I were injured, dying. I reached out to pull her near, whispered that I loved her, and mustered the last breath to kiss her for the only time...

I suddenly started awake, drenched in sweat, realizing it was all but a dream. But it was then when I realized that my love for Cherrie was more than that for a sister or close friend.

That morning, right after we had done our morning drill, I took the matter up with my cousin, Johnny Ford, also my Assistant Officer in Charge on the platoon. I began by telling him about my dream and how I realized I had feelings for Cherrie.

"You know Ted," he said when I finished, "I saw it happening before you realized it just now. All the time you spent with her, it could only come to this, marriage."

"Cherrie was never anything more than a special friend," I began. "I never considered..."

"You're blind, brother," he interrupted. "You've invested a lot in her. I know you're going to say because you care about her well-being." He stopped and looked me directly in the eye. "That's why you should marry her."

I pondered his word for a moment. "You know, you're right, I never did see it that way," I said at last. "I'm taken by surprise that my feeling for her would come to this."

"Here's another thing," Johnny continued, "I really think that marrying her would do you a lot of good. I know she was weak and insecure, but inside, she has potential to really be somebody, a teammate."

These words caught my attention, and I listened even more carefully.

"She is the one who adds colour to your life," he went on. "And you give her strength and hope. Together, I think you can be such a wonderful couple. I mean, I saw how you and her got on when you were dancing the night away at Disney World."

I continued to listen as he described what it could be like to marry her; until now, I never really planned to get married. I had never even had a girlfriend in high school. I was content as a bachelor. Cherrie was a good friend and an adopted sister. Johnny himself had been married two years ago, so I knew he had insight into the matter.

I quickly took his words to heart as we continued on with our day running our afternoon combat drills. Slowly, I began to see how things could work out for us as a couple. Inside of her, I knew she had potential as a woman and together, I could see how we could complete each other. By dinner time that evening, I had made up my mind to propose to Cherrie when we had returned.

Our Troop Commander, Robert Cleveland was the first to respond. "Well, I am pleased that you intend to do just that," he had said. "Take a week off to go home and propose to her when you return to Virginia."

I was surprised, for normally, since I had just been on leave immediately before we set off for the mission, I would have to be stationed in Virginia for the next six months until I would be granted leave again.

"Thank you sir," I responded.

"Yes," he replied. "God only knows when you could get another chance before we are called back out here. You need a chance to spend some time with her."

The rest of the men murmured in approval.

"Man, I think I want to propose to her." That was from Petty Officer Greg Grant. We all cracked up laughing.

"Well, yeah who wouldn't want to have that beautiful diamond?" added Platoon Chief Roy Roosevelt.

"There is Commander Lincoln for you," Johnny had responded sarcastically. "He goes for all the beautiful girls." I smiled and pinched at him.

"You were the one who suggested it," I replied to him with a laugh.

"Well, so you are following my orders? Well maybe I should be commander instead." We cracked up laughing again.

The rest of the evening, they continued to chatter on excitedly about my intention to propose to her. A few of them had tried laying out suggestions as to what I could do.

"Take her out to a fancy restaurant, and order a cake with the words 'Will you marry me?'"

"No, do that out in the middle of a forest, by a waterfall."

"Appear at her door all battered up, you know, the Florence Nightingale effect."

I laughed at some of their suggestions and said that I would try and think of something creative.

We have been on the field for almost four months now and were set to return home by the end of the week. I was very much looking forward to going home to my family and to see Cherrie to propose to her. But that would all change in one swift moment the following morning when suddenly the sirens sounded and immediately, everybody reported back to their respective headquarters.

As I rounded up my platoon before our HQ, I quickly did a roll call to make sure everyone was present. Commander Cleveland then relayed the message. Hostile forces had invaded one of our regional allies, and a successful coup d'état had been staged.

"It is one of the most elaborate co-ordinated schemes we have seen yet," Commander Cleveland had said. "They not only have taken hostage the administration, they also have taken over the military bases and have recruited and mobilized numerous dissidents among the civilians. They have also held hostage the local American embassy."

I could see the reaction on the faces of all the men. They were struck with disbelief, apparently all thinking the same thing. "Could this really be happening?"

"This will be a large-scale operation," Cleveland continued. "We have called in the full force of our Troop. We need everyone on hand, and we may need to stay out here for several more months."

Just then, the air raid siren had sounded and immediately we had taken cover, before strapping on our full gear and seizing our artillery.

From all around us, hostile aircraft had swarmed, firing down upon us. Our automated anti-aircraft system began firing upon them, but there was more aircraft than what the system could handle. We had to take our positions and open fire with our machine guns, before several pilots had gone airborne in their fighter planes.

With some effort, we had managed to dislodge the invaders. We had only a few casualties among our personnel, but there were many who were injured.

"The coast is clear," I had shouted when the hostile aircraft had flown off. I looked around and took a quick survey of the scene, and right away, we began taking care of the damage. We held a brief memorial service that evening for those who had been killed, storing their remains in coffins to be flown back home. The injured were taken into a makeshift hospital.

Over the following week, reinforcements had been flown into the base, and we continued to run over our objectives and formulating our strategies. We trained the guys to rehearse all different scenarios, making sure that we could be fully prepared for our strike.

Three weeks afterward, we had prepared a coordinated strike on three key bases, carried out by each of the three platoons in our troop. A Team Four platoon would also strike on a central radio tower. This attack, we determined, would grant us a strategic tactical advantage to disable the regime.

We struck well after nightfall. Boarding a stealth plane invisible to radar, we flew over to a drop point several miles from our respective targets, where we would parachute down.

Upon landing, I gathered the men in and briefed them over some final notes, and made sure we had our weapons and tools.

"This base has most of their major weapons," I had reminded them. "We have our special robot to go in before us to give the initial attack. Once inside, we need to split up into two squads. Johnny, you take your men to storm their HQ, disable their communications and capture the general overseeing the base. We will storm the artillery and shut everything down."

With that, we rose from our positions and quietly moved toward the front entrance, where a security guard stood post. Spying him through our night goggles, one of the men shot him with a silenced shot. We quickly shot down several other guards in the watchtowers above.

Another man swiftly took post inside the front entrance booth and flickering with the controls, he managed to open the front gates, before throwing a device into the central court. At that point, a swift moving machine rolled on past us and into the central court, right about where the device had been thrown. Immediately, it opened fire from its built in machine guns upon the fighter jets inside.

Naturally, the enemy got up and began attacking the machine, which had already done some damage. It was the diversion we needed. We stormed on inside amidst the confusion and upon splitting up, Johnny had swiftly stormed the central headquarters. I led the guys down into the artillery rooms.

Down inside, we had managed to find a secret laboratory, exactly what we had been looking for. Some of us marvelled in awe.

"So they do have these weapons," Roy had remarked. "Good golly."

"We need to take a sample," I announced. "Clear evidence of what we are going up against. See this?" I raised a vial of chemicals.

The men immediately set to work; while two men stood guard at the door, the rest of them began dismantling some of the special weapons inside, while picking up samples of chemicals, which we would take back to the base as evidence.

Suddenly, an alarm had sounded. We quickly pulled our masks back on and levelled our weapons, just as armed men came storming on inside, opening fire upon us. Their bullets, however, were impervious against our bullet-proof suits and we subdued them.

As we emerged from the underground bunkers, the base had been thrown into total confusion, for Johnny had managed to capture the overseeing officer before firing on some of the other men.

Staying low, we had managed to set off a charge of explosives right before one of our helicopters had arrived. We quickly boarded, taking along our prisoner, before making off back to our base.

Upon our arrival, I quickly produced the samples of chemicals we had salvaged to Commander Cleveland and the other officers in charge.

"Biological warfare," Cleveland had remarked on seeing these chemicals. "We need to get this into our labs for further testing. See if it is the real thing. But meanwhile, that is objective one down."

They had taken in the prisoner for questioning, attempting to get him to reveal the whereabouts of the hostages. Meanwhile, with the enemy's militia having taken a hit, we continued to plan our next move.

We were on the field for two more years. The entire situation would become an ongoing conflict that could run on into the foreseeable future. Riots have broken out among civilians as the dissidents had been exposed. That gave way to their militia coming in and attacking them, which we immediately countered by moving in our forces.

In time however, we had managed to oust the regime from the capitol and immediately, we had set about installing an interim government and quickly, reconstruction had begun. We dismantled our temporary base and moved into the city, occupying one of their military bases. However, the mission was far from over, for there were still many insurgents among the civilians causing trouble.

I can still see it vividly. People were being shot and killed, by the militia, but even more at the hands of other civilians. In all my years of service, I have never witnessed bloodshed on this scale. Clearly, we were up against an adversary that knows no respect for human life. I can still see the flow of blood and the screams of the dying and the hostile cries for bloodshed still plague my mind.

Chapter 4

AFTER THE TIME HAD passed, our entire platoon had been returned to home base in Virginia. On landing, I was immediately granted leave. I took a hot shower, a nice, which was nice and refreshing especially after having gone without one for many days. I then packed my bags and then caught a taxi to the airport, from where I would fly home on our family jet.

To say that I was happy to be coming home is an understatement. I had been overwhelmed emotionally to have witnessed the atrocities I had seen. People were dying needlessly, in my mind, butchering each other over their conflicts. This was war like we never seen before. It was a dark and hopeless world, and it still disturbs me to know these things take place. "And here I am, sitting cozy half a world away in America while in another world, people butcher each other," I thought to myself. "I got to do something, but what?"

Tammy was waiting for me at the airport. Immediately on seeing her, I dropped my bags as she rushed forward and we hugged each other. Never before had I been so overjoyed to see my sister again.

"Welcome home," Tammy was saying. "We heard about the onset of war, and were so worried about you."

"It was such a frightening event," I responded, releasing them to pick up my bags and we made our way out to the parking lot. "It disturbs me every time I see this happening. I wondered if I would ever see your pretty face again."

I picked up my bags and we got onboard the plane which sat in the runway. Before long, we were airborne, en route back to Michigan.

Normally, I would have been exhausted after enduring such an arduous mission. But right now, as I looked outside at the clear blue skies, just knowing that I was home again, here in the land of the free, I was beginning to feel reinvigorated.

We landed in Michigan about three hours later. As we returned home and I got out and gathered my bags from and came through the front door, we were greeted by a crowd waiting inside.

"SURPRISE!!!"

On the second floor banisters above the foyer, I noticed a "Welcome Home" banner. Balloons and streamers were decorated across the whole room. The entire foyer was crowded, and there were people on the stairs and the balcony above.

I recognized most of the people. They were mostly friends and relatives, along with other co-workers and board members from the company. And on the balcony, front and center, were my parents smiling proudly at me.

I was glad that I had showered before arriving to a party, because having gone many days without one left my body feeling like a solid block of slime.

The crowd parted to make way, as I moved through the foyer and up the winding staircase, smiling and greeting people with a hug or a shake of the hand, until I made it to the top where my folks were waiting. They rushed out and engulfed me in their arms for a long moment.

"Welcome home son," my mother said tearfully. "We're proud of you."

Never before had I been so excited to see my folks before. It seemed like an eternity has gone by, being away from my family and loved ones. I leaned over and kissed her cheek.

"We have a surprise for you, son," my father added, as they released me.

Right behind them stood Cherrie and Marie.

"Cherrie!" I beamed, reaching out and embracing her tightly. "So good to see you again," I added.

"Welcome home, soldier," she replied.

I released her from her grasp and then greeted her mother with a hug. "Marie," I greeted, "Oh what a surprise you see you both here."

"We had to come over to welcome you back," she said. "Tammy flew down and rushed us up here. And you young man have another call of duty to attend to."

"I will take care of that," I promised.

I spent the next thirty minutes circulating through the crowd, greeting everyone. The whole house seemed to be filled to the brim, from the foyer to the kitchen and adjacent family room. It seemed like nearly everyone I knew was there.

Most of the time, Cherrie was right by my side when I was going about through the crowd. It was so packed out, with everyone coming to talk to me, that I didn't have time to propose to her. I could not wait to get her alone so I could perform "the call of duty" as her mother called it.

"Just like that party you threw for me," Cherrie had been saying to me, as we all made our way to the back yard where dinner was being served. "Just about everyone you know, here to welcome you back."

"This means a lot," I replied. "I miss every one of you so much, being out there."

"You done it for all of us, Ted," she replied, "our family, our neighbours, our whole country."

Our back yard was also decorated, with floating balloons strung from the garden. The scarecrow was dressed in military garb. Lawn chairs and blankets were scattered throughout the yard, allowing plenty of seating space.

Having gathered my serving, I sat down in a lawn chair near the center of the yard. The designated "seat of honour" as they called it. I was joined by my family, as well as Cherrie and Marie. Throughout dinner, more people kept coming up to us to welcome me home.

As the sun went down, we built a fire and everyone gathered around roasting marshmallows and s'mores. Tammy pulled out her guitar and began singing camp songs, with everyone joining in before I began telling my story.

I started with my departure and then continued to describe my daily duties. I mentioned a few brief highlights during the mission, leading up to the climax, the ensuing attack that kept me away for another seven months. I left out the part of the dream, feeling it was a private matter between Cherrie and me.

"It was probably the most intense moment of my life," I'd concluded. "But being out there revealed to me just how much I've come to value each and every one of you and why I'm proud to represent you in our nation's fight for freedom worldwide."

The crowd nodded in agreement and gave applause when I finished. With that, we adjourned from the camp fire and guests began to disperse, some gathering in the kitchen or rear patio, while others went to the rec room.

I went upstairs to change into my swim wear, and took a dip in our swimming pool along with several other guests. Having been in on the mission for many days, it was especially refreshing diving into the cool water and feeling stiff arms and legs reinvigorated.

A little later, Cherrie also came out and took a dip in the pool. "Are you following me?" I joked, when we had swum into the shallower waters and stood up.

She laughed. "Just because I'm also taking a dip to cool off?" she replied. "Great minds think alike." Suddenly turning a pleading eye, she added, "Your family says you've a surprise for me. I want to know what that is."

Still a little jovial, I responded, "Surprise? I have a surprise for you?"

"Com'on Ted."

I smiled and then said, "Later, when we're alone."

The rest of the night went on by, with more events around the house. I joined some of the guys down in the rec room to play a round of billiards. Later, after most of the guests had left, I sat down with Cherrie and a few other friends of ours to watch a movie.

The next morning, I took Cherrie out walking at Rouge Park where I told her about my dream of her, how she unexpectedly turned up, having been taken hostage, only to be rescued by me. I told her about how she had begged me to stay with her, and how at the end, we were both gunned down and then kissed with our dying breath.

Cherrie was moved to tears when I concluded my story. "Oh, oh, that's so tragic if that really happened," she said.

"It would be," I agreed. "But Cherrie..." I stopped, pulled her aside, and put my arm around her. "Cherrie, it was here when my eyes were really opened, that I love you. I love you, more than as a little sister or a good friend."

Cherrie was visibly surprised. "What are you saying?" she asked.

It was then when I knelt and pulled out my ring box. "Cherrie," I continued, "I don't just want to be there for you. I love you and I want to be with you forever. Cherrie Lopez-Harrison, will you marry me?"

For a while, she was speechless, and then I saw her gradually break into tears again. She wept for nearly two minutes, unable to speak. I pulled her forward and kissed her forehead.

"I do," she finally said through her tears. "I'm sorry, I don't know why I'm crying, but yes, I will marry you."

I took her by the hand and slid the ring onto her finger, and then pulled her close, embracing her tightly and kissing her gently on the forehead.

We held an engagement party the following evening, back at the house again. This was a more formal event, and guests came out in tuxedos and dresses. Again, people were coming up to us, congratulating our engagement and wishing us the best.

Cherrie openly shared my story of dreaming about her being held hostage only to be rescued by me, and how that dream opened my eyes. She called that a classic love story.

Later, Tammy called everyone out to the back patio, but invited Cherrie and I to sit in the gazebo adjacent to the pool. I wondered what was going on as we made our way over, having a feeling that something was up.

"I just wanted to offer my greatest congratulations to my new sister in law, Cherrie Lopez-Harrison Lincoln," she began with a flourish. Everyone applauded.

"But," Tammy continued, "a wedding is going to be a real wedded matter, so I better warn her what she's about to face." Turning to Cherrie, she added, "Cherrie, push the red button at your feet."

Everyone must have cringed, knowing she was up to something. Cherrie looked up. "What are you up to here?" she asked.

"Just push the button or I'll do it for you."

With hesitation, Cherrie reached with her toes, stepping on the button. Suddenly the floor fell beneath her and she tumbled down onto a small slide and into the pool.

"What is a wedding if you don't get wet?" Tammy concluded.

The crowd was visibly shocked, and Cherrie was initially livid, but she soon lightened up and began to laugh as she swam over and got out of the pool.

"You dirty rat!" I exploded sarcastically. "How about I push you in?"

"Do it!" she replied. "And jump in yourself!"

Whipping off my jacket and shoes, I picked her up and threw her into the pool, before jumping in myself. It wasn't before long when other guests began jumping into the pool, still wearing their formal dinner wear.

For a moment, I regretted what I started, but nobody seemed to care too much. Somehow, they were becoming children just once more. That seemed to happen every time Cherrie was around; her child-like air was contagious and even my military-bred family wasn't immune to it.

Chapter 5

I LEARNED ABOUT HARRY Madison's interest in Cherrie, when Jimmy Truman, an old friend from Navy academy, warned me that Harry was very much after her. He had come to visit us at the base in Virginia, where I had been stationed after a year-long tour of duty since having gotten engaged.

He told me about everything the guy had done, from leaving notes for her at the locker rooms to trying to hunt her down after games. "He is taking no prisoners, stalking your girl," he was saying. "He doesn't care about the fact that Cherrie is off the market. He is determined to woo her."

I laughed a little bit. "Unfortunately, I don't blame him. I am not surprised because a lot of guys would want her. But as long as she can resist him..."

"That is right, but she is terrified."

"I can imagine that. Well, I will keep talking to her and reassuring her."

The most atrocious act he had done was getting one of her friends drunk and getting her to reveal Cherrie's phone number. Fortunately, since she was visiting me up in Virginia, losing Harry was simple; we switched phones. Predictably, I did get a call from Harry.

Inside, I wanted to sock the guy for stalking her, but I restrained my emotions. On top of being jealous for her attention and faithfulness, I was concerned that she could easily be taken advantage of, and was frustrated that I could not be around to protect her honour. Instead, I encouraged her to be strong and stand up for herself.

Marie's wedding that year worried me. I knew about her relationship with John Hoover, a man whom I have little respect for; I sensed in him, a decadent, controlling man who is merely interested in absorbing her business into his empire, while landing the beautiful woman.

As I came into the mess hall for breakfast one morning, there on the table I saw a magazine with a front cover picture of Cherrie and Harry making out.

"Well, well, your girl's gone with another guy," Roy had said, trying to hide a smirk.

"Unbelievable," said my cousin Johnny, shaking his head.

I took the magazine, looking closer at it, staring in disbelief and jealousy. Wordlessly, I excused myself and went back to my quarters.

Sitting down at my desk, I picked up a picture of Cherrie, one that sat framed on my desk, looking longingly into her eyes. I then pulled out my phone and called her up.

"Hello?" her voice came.

"Cherrie," I said, "Hey Cherrie, are you there?"

"Yes," she replied, her voice muffled, "I am here."

I could detect a sense of guilt in her voice and decided I would let her bring up the matter. "Are you okay?" I asked. "You don't sound well."

"I guess you heard the news," she said. "I was caught on camera with Harry."

"I heard the news. Saw a magazine cover."

"I am so sorry Ted. I was drunk that evening, unable to handle mommy suddenly getting married. And I let my guard down, and before I knew it, he kissed me." Her voice was ever more gripped with fear and guilt.

"Did he also propose to you?" I added.

"I didn't tell him yes," she responded. "I mean, I was joking around, but we had too much to drink. I was so drunk I didn't know what was happening; if I were sober, I would have told him no. In fact, I didn't know he was in love with me."

I paused for a moment and gave thought to her words. "I'm not surprised," I finally said. "I figured Harry wanted you. But Cherrie, I'm disappointed you dropped your guard."

"I'm sorry! I'm so sorry! Please forgive me for what I've done." Her voice broke down and she wept.

Again, I paused and let her shed her tears. Now, more than ever, my heart longed for her; I knew she wanted to do good, but was still flailing about. I wanted to change that as soon as possible.

"I made a foolish mistake," she continued. "I feel like that rebellious little girl all over again, one who hung out with the cool kids, drifted away from you, and got into big trouble. I am ashamed of myself for not learning from my mistakes." She sobbed again, and then added, "But I love you too, if you still love me. You have every right to just end our engagement right now."

I sighed and for a moment, I said nothing. I had been appalled that Harry Madison had taken advantage of my fiancée, whom I knew was defenseless. Listening to her sobbing voice, I could tell that she was sincerely sorry about what had happened, and more than ever, my heart longed for her.

"Cherrie," I finally said, "Cherrie, I love you too much to let you go. I know you made a big mistake, but I won't let that change anything. It will be over soon." I paused again and taking a glimpse at my calendar, I added, "We could get married next month when I have leave."

"Next month? Ted are you serious?"

"Sure, we can get our plans arranged." Inside, I was already trying to see how our plans could unfold. "I will talk to my superiors to see if I can get the leave to plan for a wedding."

Right after talking to her, I realized I had made an arbitrary promise. The good news was that we had gone over the guest list and other ware. However, we still did not arrange for a venue for the ceremony. I only had one week off, and it was unrealistic to have everything come together on such short notice.

"I can understand why you would want to do this," Commander Cleveland had been saying when I reported to his office. "And frankly, I want you to get married before you fly out again."

"Thank you, sir," I replied, surprised.

"So I am going to arrange for you to get married here in Virginia," he went on. "We can set up the venue and pay for expenses to have it set up. Lord knows when you will have a chance to see her again."

I was beaming from ear to ear as I left his office and on returning to my quarters, I called up my family.

"We could have a wedding date set," I had been saying. "They want to host the wedding here in Virginia, before I leave."

When we arrived back in Virginia, I had learned that preparations had been made. I got to see where the wedding will be held, in a park. The men worked around the clock to set up the site where the wedding was held. The aim was to create "a secluded paradise," and we picked an ideal location, in an orchard grove surrounded by a forest on one side. A small creek ran through the area, complementing the scenery.

I met up with Cherrie and our attendants, making sure everything else was in order, from the guest list to the schedule of events. It was hectic, given how rapidly everything was going together, but we were getting things done.

Since her father was still out of the picture, Cherrie had asked my father to give her away. It looked like a strange situation, but this was a testimony of how she has become part of our family.

Just before big day, I went to fetch Cherrie early in the morning from the guest suite, bringing her down to look at the wedding site. She was visibly stunned when she saw the beautiful setting, down in a field surrounded by an orchard grove. However, I somehow could sense in her a feeling of reservation.

"Something just doesn't seem right," she had said when I asked her about it. "Maybe I am just over sensitive. But I am somewhat worried about getting married so soon. Why, I don't know."

Right away, my mind began to tell me that something wasn't right, that perhaps we should call off the wedding. That didn't sit too well in my heart though, for I was anxious to get married before flying off again. What if something happened to me while on the field? Besides, we had already pushed ahead with our plans, it felt too late to turn back now.

Regardless, I went with my head. "My dove," I said to her, "I love you so much, and I will do whatever you feel is right."

She thought about it, and then decided to proceed with the wedding.

The big day arrived after much hassle and preparation, and everything was set up for what was to be her dream wedding. We had almost six hundred guests in attendance. Family members and friends had come from all across the country to witness the grand moment, something that the press would not get to witness. Thanks to the military providing security, we were able to seal out the ever-intrusive press.

As I stood eagerly at the altar, while her bridesmaids filed forth, I was thinking back over the years I'd known the girl, from the time we had taken her and her mother into our family. I thought of our time we'd spent growing up together until they moved to Florida. I remembered crying with her when they had to move, knowing that we'd be living apart for the first time since her infancy. I recalled all the times we'd spent together, from our high school years and onward, right up to when I proposed to her.

We had appreciated and savoured every precious moment we could be together. The times apart were bound to continue, at least until my time of service would be complete. But once we got married, in spirit, she would no longer be alone.

Finally, Cherrie appeared at the rear, accompanied by my father. The entire crowd stood at attention as they filed forward. I locked my eyes with hers, my heart racing with excitement. We would be married very soon.

As she came closer, however, I began to notice her facial expression through the veil. If I were not mistaken, I thought she was beginning to get cold feet. I shrugged it off, hoping I was wrong.

It turned out, I was not wrong, for as soon as they reached the altar, Cherrie suddenly turned and bolted out.

Everyone was stunned to silence by the sudden turn of events. Never before had I seen so many shocked faces, as though they had witnessed a suicide bombing in front of them. The silence was suddenly broken with a scream from the front of the crowd. All hell suddenly broke loose. Some people were sobbing, others screaming. I was then immediately surrounded by a crowd of family members and friends.

Inside, I was beginning to feel deeply cut from within by her sudden betrayal. I was suddenly added to her list of deserted men, and this time, it was right at the altar. All the years she'd grown up with me, confided in me, and all, it suddenly came to naught at this moment. Overwhelmed, I excused myself and left.

Chapter 6

IF IT HADN'T BEEN ANY clearer in the past, I realized now just how much I loved and cared about her. The emptiness I felt in my heart was a gap I knew I could never fill. After returning to the base that afternoon, I had taken a short stroll through the complex.

Inside, I had found myself growing bitter and angry with Cherrie's betrayal. After all I had invested in her, for her to turn and run away like that, it was inconceivable and selfish.

But yet, on the other hand, there was a part of me that still loved her and had compassion for her even though she had done me wrong. That side of me had asked what I may have done to cause things to go wrong. "Did I push too soon to get married?" I wondered.

Never before had I been in a state of anxiety and confusion. Before, I had always been able to look above my problems and somehow keep a level head amidst the consternation, but this time, I was up against a powerful force that would potentially send my life spiralling.

The following morning we had boarded the plane to return to the field. While onboard, we had received word about the whereabouts of the exiled terrorist leaders. Our next objective was to capture them and take them prisoners. "This could be the final step in the mission," Cleveland had been saying. "With this last blow, we can begin to restore order and restore the administration."

I looked over the maps and diagrams. After all of the previous missions we had been fighting, I thought this one seemed fairly straight forward, for they were not hiding in a rocky cleft, but they were staying in a civilian complex. "We have them checkmated," I agreed.

We set out only two days after reconvening at the base. I decided that we may as well strike while the iron was hot, before they got wise to us and flew the coup. It would however prove to be a mistake, for inside, I was still reeling emotionally from Cherrie's sudden desertion and was prone to make mistakes.

The complex was on an island a few miles offshore, so we flew out there in our stealth plane. I instructed the pilot where to drop us. Splitting into two teams again, I put one team under Johnny, instructing him to remain in the air and back us up. "Make sure you stay out of visual contact," I reminded them, before I led the team on the initial insertion.

We plunged down and parachuting at the last moment, we plunged into the water, before swimming on up to the complex. Climbing out of the water, we carefully surveyed the area and then cautiously made our way toward the main building, weapons in hand. We stopped and hid behind a rock.

As we regrouped and made our preparations to break in, I suddenly realized that we had neglected to bring our SATCOM radios to signal to the other team.

"Nuts," I had said. "I hate to say it, but we are going to be alone without our backup team. Change in plans, I need three men to scale the back wall and break into the window. Two of you stay on guard in case something should happen. The rest of you, be prepared to storm the front entrance." At that point, we unpacked our equipment and got to work.

As I scaled up the wall, pick in hand, I said a quiet prayer, hoping I could be successful in executing the mission, for I knew I was slipping. I quietly pulled up next to the window, and using my heat sensing device, I could make out someone sleeping. This, I had gathered, was the general who led the coup, now in exile.

With lightning speed, I smashed my pick into the window, before jumping in. As the man awoke and whipped out a gun, I whipped out my TASER gun and knocked him out. I swiftly bound the general as my men came in and hurled him toward the window.

Suddenly, armed men had stormed into the room. I ordered my men to take our prisoner out the window, while I would hold the men back. As the guys swarmed around me, I quickly leapt upon two of the men, knocking them down with a series of one-two punches. Many more swarmed around behind me, but I quickly moved to tackle them before knocking down the man in front of me before leaping right upon the shoulders of one of the men and then jumping again back toward the window.

"You guys can kill me right now," I said to them, "but it is over now."

A commotion arose outside. Apparently, alarm had been raised that we had raided the complex and they were on all of us. Gunfire had erupted. I slid down the rope, before whipping out my gun again. But before I could open fire, chloroform began rising up from the ground. I suddenly realized that we did not bring our gas masks, another bad mistake. We were soon knocked out.

When I had awoken, I could see we were tossed into a dungeon. The room was so cramped, that we were made to lie atop of one another.

"This is it," I said to myself. I was unable to believe that I could have made such a big mistake. The men outside the base were probably scattering about, trying to find us, while we were locked inside. An entire platoon had failed its mission and had only managed to get itself captured and held hostage. And it was entirely my fault for losing my mind at such a critical moment.

None of my men said anything to me. In our military training, we were disciplined never to question our superiors even when they make poor decisions. But as of now, I didn't care if they did question me. I would have deserved it.

After several hours, they had dragged me out of the dungeon and set me in front of a camera.

"We have in custody, a platoon commander with the United States Special Warfare Department," the ringleader had said, smirking into the camera. "Your most elite military division is now held hostage, unable to protect and serve as you claim. Your forces for justice has become but fodder."

He stuck me across the face. "Is this what you Americans rely on to protect you?" he continued. He then kicked me in the waist.

"Your protection is gone," the man went on. "There is no one who can protect you now. We will proceed with our operations and we will have full control over the entire region. From here, we can launch a full force against America and annihilate you. Anyone who comes against us shall be like this rag doll of what you call a tough soldier."

We were tortured greatly over the next few days. I overheard one of the men suggest that they simply kill us, but the leader said that we would be used to fulfill another purpose. I was dragged out and they injected me with something. My vision began to cloud, and then my mind went blank and I fell over.

All of a sudden, as it seemed, I awoke again and everything was gradually coming back into focus. My head still ringing, I managed to get out of bed. Emerging from my quarters, I soon encountered Commander Cleveland.

"Another ally is now held under siege," he had said. "The enemy had captured it in a coup d'état. We need you to dislodge the insurgents."

Something still didn't feel right, but I didn't know what it was. I was certain that I had just been captured on my last strike. Or was it a dream?

"I have a headache," I said, clutching my head which was still ringing. He gave me a pill with a glass of water. I thanked him and took the pill. Gradually, my vision began to clear up and my mind became more active.

Before long, I had rounded up my men. After going over roll call as usual, I inspected them, made sure we were armed and ready for our strike.

"Another target has been hit," I had said. "The enemy has taken down an ally. They installed a false government in a coup. We need to strike now to take them out."

"Yes, sir," they responded in unison.

It was beginning to feel normal again. Perhaps everything was just a terrible nightmare. We boarded a plane and made off for our target. I had referred to the map that Cleveland had given me, taking note of where we were to parachute.

As we flew along, my mind darted back to Cherrie again. At first I grimaced in frustration, but somehow, deep inside my heart, I still found myself longing for her, eager to hold her hand once again. "Why do I still feel this way?" I wondered. "She had left me, why do I still care?"

I was disturbed by my feelings. "Has Cherrie got a hold of me?" I asked myself. "Come now, Ted, don't let her take over everything, or you will never get out of this emotional prison." Angrily, I fought back against my feelings. "Get over her now. She is a betrayer who took everything you had." I clenched my fist and my jaws, and at that moment, if I saw her right before me...

My thoughts were interrupted as we suddenly came upon the target. As we circled overhead the capitol, I instructed my men to get their parachutes ready and we jumped.

We landed down upon the roof of the building. Pulling out our heat sensing devices, I could make out where everyone was below us. Once we found the executive chambers, I instructed the men to strike on them. Attaching ropes on the roof, we then swung down, smashing through the windows, before brandishing our guns on the occupants inside the room.

"Meeting is over, imposters," I yelled, raising the gun. "You can do this the easy way or the hard way. Get up and leave quietly."

At first, there was no response, just a shocked look, before the president, sitting at the far end, pushed for a buzzer and then stood up. "Meeting adjourned," he told the others. He calmly made his way toward me.

"You can put down that gun," he continued. "You can throw us out, but justice will be served."

I stared him down, before motioning for my men to bind them up and lead them out.

We were suddenly interrupted by a large force of security guards who came busting into the door, surrounding us. I turned swiftly and socked the nearest one, before turning and firing the gun up at the ceiling.

"Traitors, all of you!" I yelled. "Come to the aid of your country and dislodge these offenders."

As we began engaging the guards in a fight, more armed men came bursting in behind them, opening fire. Half of the guards quickly turned and hustled the president and his cabinet out of the room, while the other half turned to fight the new intruders.

It was only then, when the spell was broken and I realized that I had been drugged. I was not dispatched by Commander Cleveland following a nightmare; it was the other way around. My men had been captured and held hostage, then re-programmed to attack another regional ally.

But it was too late now, for by now, they had hauled everyone out of the room and have taken them hostage. As for us, well there was no escape.

The terrorists had successfully taken over the government and having procured popular support from key insurgents amongst civilians and the militia, embarked on genocide of the ethnic residents in this country.

My men and I were imprisoned. Rather than killing us, I realized they intended to use us to fulfill their objectives. They continued to torture and drug us, in hopes that this could break us down and brainwash us. And they were beginning to succeed, for by now, I had begun to forget who I was. My human emotions were gone, replaced by a raw determination to unleash fury upon a target. I was being transformed into a pit bull, a killing machine, without human emotions.

Already, they had released me or one of my men from prison, sending us out to go assassinate certain people in public – all while filming the event, which I later learned was shown on American television. American SEALs were now programmed by the enemy to kill our allies as part of their systematic genocide. The sight could only be highly discouraging to people at home.

Several weeks had unfolded. I was lying asleep one evening when a prison guard I didn't recognize came on in. I awoke and sat up, looking on him with a scowl.

"It's okay, just lie down." The man's voice was unusually reassuring and I lay down again, wondering if it were a trick. Could he be one of their hypnotist specialists?

He stood over me and rubbed my aching shoulders, before injecting me with a needle, and gradually, my thoughts began to clear up and my emotions were beginning to return.

Just a few hours later, another guard had unlocked my cell door and led me out to the larger room, sitting me down before several other terrorists. "We think we can use you for yet another strike," the chief guard had begun. "We will send you to go and quash a certain resistance, hiding out at this base."

Pretending to still be under the influence of the drugs, I growled and began swinging my hands. Someone grabbed my arm.

"Yes, yes," he said reassuringly. "Go kill them. We'll take you there.

In less than an hour, my men and I were herded into a delivery truck to go and "hunt down" their targets, which included an American ambassador and several local government officials who had gone off into hiding. As we rolled along, carted in the back with no one to guard us, I quickly told the men about our plans.

"We've just been set free," I said. "Now we need to come up with some plot to break away from these guys." With that, my men, also de-drugged, began coming up with different stages of our plans.

Before long, the truck had come to a halt and, resuming pretense, we became animals, as a captor came striding in. "The hideout is in there," he said, pointing at a mouth of a cave. "We have tracked them down. Go arrest them and bring them out."

No sooner had he finished speaking when we stormed out and into the cave. Naturally, the occupants inside were taken by surprise, and we easily overpowered them, bound them, and hauled them out. Before long, we were all back inside the back of the truck.

As the truck began moving, I soon unmasked and began untying our prisoners. "You are free," I told them. "We got to come out with our plan."

In the corner were a stack of weapons. Naturally, the captors thought they were safe to leave them here with bound up prisoners and a pack of animals without a will of their own. I pulled out the carton and before long everyone was clad in battle gear, with guns and bullet proof armour. The whole idea was to come out and attack the captors before storming in and dislodging the remainder of our captors.

The whole plan was successful. Naturally, when the truck came to a stop, we gunned them down easily when they opened the door. We proceeded into the prison complex, storming the terrorists inside, we slew them off before releasing some more military and political prisoners, including the prime minister and president of the country.

Convening out in the larger room, we then formulated our final objective, to storm the capitol and dislodge the enemy leaders. We struck that evening, sneaking through a secret entryway, we rapidly captured the enemy leaders and before long, we had restored the nation's leaders.

There was still more work to be done, for we had to restore order amongst the insurgents who had supported the coup. American forces were called in, and loyal citizens, including an organized underground resistance, were quickly mobilized. After about three months, order was restored.

By now, we were flying back home to Virginia. I had resigned from my post with the Navy, for I had found I could no longer keep up with the demanding duties. My last blunder was especially costly, and as we learned from the media, was a major blow to the morale of the military, all because I had made one major misstep in forgetting to bring two crucial items.

But it was here when I realized I was up against a much higher power and had to re-evaluate who was really in charge of my own life, me or someone else?

Chapter 7

TWO DAYS AFTER RETURNING to Virginia, I was sent over
to a camp down in Puerto Rico, a rehabilitation camp for ex-militia,
to get them re-habilitated into society. The camp was located on
the northwest shore, a relatively secluded area overlooking the
beachfront. There were several cabins organized around a central
"square" where everyone stayed.

The traumas of war can do a surprising number on soldiers who
have gone through it, and tragically, many of them spend the rest of
their days imprisoned in a pit of depression and despair, unable to
re-connect with society. A lot end up committing suicide.

There were several "workshops" held that afternoon, where
different counsellors met with attendees, teaching them on how to
get re-integrated. After having unpacked, I went out to meet with
a couple of counsellors about life. When I had talked with them
about my experiences, they began counselling me over what kinds
of changes to expect. They were helpful in helping me get over the
traumas of war, but there was still this gap in my life which remained,
made all the worse with Cherrie's departure.

After dinner, we all gathered in the central square for a message
from the camp director, Harold Jefferson, a former major in the
Navy, who now serves as a missionary in some of the poor and
war-torn areas where he had toured during his militia service.

I groaned at first, when he pulled out his Bible. Inside, I was
screaming, "What good is God anyway? He is either a weakling or
a total fraud." I was very bitter after all I had to endure and I almost
wanted to get up and walk away, but some unknown force kept me
seated where I was.

"But they that wait upon the LORD shall renew their strength;
they shall mount up with wings as eagles," he had begun. "They shall

run, and not be weary; and they shall walk and not faint. Isaiah 40:31."

Those words caught my attention, and I sat up, listening in more intently as he carried on.

"Brothers and sisters, we are in a mission of spiritual warfare, wherever it may be. Spirits transcend that of flesh and blood, and thus there is nothing you can do in your own power."

There were several murmurs of agreement from the attendees, and even I couldn't help but agree. He smiled and carried on with his talk.

"Is there any of you who is faint or weary?" he went on. "Well God in Heaven goes before you. He will grant you power in your time of need and strength for when you go forth." With that, he concluded his speech with an alter call, inviting people to come forward to be saved.

Inside of me, the internal resistance I had melted away and before I realized it, I was down on my knees praying with Jefferson and the dozens of other attendees. As I prayed, somehow, I began to feel a sudden change; a deep warmth had swept over me. I was free from the depression, the missing gap in my life was gone. I pulled myself up and wiping my face off, I just knelt and listened to a voice I could hear deep inside of me.

"If you want to do something about the world you had seen," the inner voice seemed to be saying, "follow Me, for I have a plan for you."

Once again, I was feeling stronger and more fulfilled. The old resentments, burdens, embarrassment, it was all gone now that I had re-committed my life to Christ for the first time since I had made my first profession as a child. I was the prodigal son who had come home after having been faced with the real depravity of life. It was now time for me to give my life over to His service.

That evening, they had me doing night watch duty after everyone had gone to bed. I would spend the night patrolling the grounds, making sure everything was stored away and no trouble emerged. Out in the distance, I could hear the pounding surf ebb away as I made my rounds to the different places he had asked me to check. Make sure everything was secure and nothing was lying around.

As I was making my way through one point, near a low bluff, suddenly a car had come roaring off from the bluff and crashing down to the ground before spinning over to a standstill. I made my way over to the car, flashing my light in her direction.

"Whoever you are, identify yourself," I called out as I approached. "This is private property."

"I'm sorry," I could hear a female voice reply. "I was trying to get away..."

I immediately recognized the voice. "Cherrie?" I began.

"Ted?" she responded. "Oh, no, no."

Cherrie was still sitting in the car. "I'm sorry, I'm sorry," was all she could say.

Despite having been hurt by her betrayal, inside, I could not help but feel compassion for her. I quickly opened the door for her. As she tried to get out, she winced in pain.

"I'm injured," she said. "My back has been compressed and I think I have a whiplash to the head."

Very gently, I reached inside, pulling her out of the car, making sure her head was resting on my shoulder, and carried her back to the camp.

"My baby girl," I said to her, "you left me at the altar, alone in front of everyone. Am I but another guy you felt you had to deceive?"

"I'm so sorry," she said. "I was caught in a tangled web of emotions." She proceeded to tell me her story, explaining that she was feeling rushed into marriage so soon and was beginning to feel more intimidated as she came to the altar. She ran off because she felt unprepared to get married so soon.

"I'm sorry too," I responded. "I think I overreacted and made a decision I didn't realize would put you in a compromising situation."

"Ted, will you please forgive me?" The tears in her eyes only yanked at my heart, and suddenly, I had no choice but to say yes.

"Cherrie, I forgive you." Suddenly, like a bolt of lightning, love surged back into my heart, and I took a deep breath. I held her even tighter and kissed her cheek.

"I promise you, I am never, ever, ever going to leave you like I did," Cherrie continued. "And if you do reject me, well, I am going to feed myself to the sharks."

"You don't have to do that," I replied. "I can tell you how to find new life." Just now, we reached the medical building. Kicking open the door, I brought her inside, and then went to fetch someone for help.

Looking back, I realized that God had brought us both to this point to break us down and bring us back to Him. He brought her into my life to teach me about the reality of love, and then took her away briefly to show me His grace. Now it was time for us to come back together in Him.

Several weeks had gone by and we were at the altar once again, back in Detroit, before a crowd of relatives, close friends, and even some of my former colleagues. Once again, Cherrie had come down the aisle with my father, this time, she was firmly committed to getting married and running the race with me. The ceremony carried on through its entirety and the minister pronounced us "husband and wife," and we kissed before everyone.

As we came out however, deputies had suddenly arrived and whisked her off. "Mrs. Madison," their chief had said, "I'm going to ask you to come with us. We have you on charge for matrimonial bigamy."

I was stunned by the sudden turn of events, for she had told me nothing about getting married to Harry Madison when we went to the altar. But as we sat before our counsellor to discuss our legal options, he had casually suggested annulment.

"It is the easiest route to put the matter behind us," he said. "If you have not consummated your marriage, you can take this route."

She smiled and agreed to that option. "I have found my man and I'm sticking with him," she had said.

Interlogue

THE ROOM WAS MOVED deeply after hearing Lincoln's story, and there was a respectful silence when he finished. That did not last long, for after he had taken his seat, reporters were buzzing once more. There were legal implications in Cherrie's marrying someone while she was already engaged to another man, and with this latest story, she was potentially now in deeper waters.

As Lincoln took his seat, before the judge could ask prosecutor Monroe to call upon another witness, suddenly a young, red-haired woman burst into the courtroom, running down to the stand, followed by three well-dressed men.

"Where is Harry Madison?" she was demanding.

"Young lady, you are interrupting a case in session," the judge responded sternly. "Please leave now, or face charges of contempt of court."

"I contempt court with a case of my own!" the woman screamed out. "These are my counselors and I am here to press charges against Harry Madison for breach of marital engagement. I demand that I be allowed to speak."

The crowd was now beside themselves with shock with yet another turn of events, this time, involving the plaintiff, who now could be charged with a crime of breach of marital engagement himself. They soon quieted and listened in, as the judge granted the floor to the newcomer, recognized as Dorothy Reagan, a California actress and businesswoman.

Dorothy's story: Chapter 1

"I DON'T GET NO SATISFACTION," is a line by the Rolling Stones in their famous song. Frankly, that song couldn't describe a person's life better. Who can find satisfaction? Nobody! No matter how hard you work, how much you strive, happiness and satisfaction eludes you like a fleeting dream.

Growing up in a blue-collar family in Chicago, I felt pressure to become someone. I worked hard in school every day. During the summer, I had an interest in business, running a stand for lemonade and baked goods. I steadily grew my business and before long, I was able to buy new clothes and keep up with the latest fashions.

While I enjoyed business, my dream had been acting. My mother had been a small-time actor herself, and I adopted her love for drama and performing. She was fully supportive of my quest and pushed me to work at my craft. Together, we shared a dream that I would somehow vindicate her flop and emerge as a famous actress.

I took additional after-school drama lessons and worked hard every day. But try as I may, I could never seem to break through. I was overweight and not pretty thus I was often passed over for many of the good roles.

I can still recall my freshman year, when I auditioned to star in A Midsummer Night's Dream, my favourite play. I had often jabbered on with my friends about doing this.

"You go do this, girl." That was from Roberta Pierce, my best friend, someone who had always been there for me, no matter how bad things got. We were in the cafeteria over lunch, and I was preparing for the audition, which was held the following week.

"Well, I am counting on this," I replied. "I have worked my tail off for this role day in and day out." I went on talking about how I had often been passed over good roles in my earlier years.

Roberta was someone I really envied. She was pretty and as a result, got many of the good roles in the school drama. She was on numerous school clubs, from yearbook to the cheerleading squad. She was on the "in crowd" of the cool students. And yet, somehow she still befriended me, though I was an outsider. Right now, she was listening to me as I poured out my concerns and frustrations.

"I know things can be somewhat unfair," she had said. "But even I have learned that you cannot hinge your entire self-worth on making it as an actress."

"I know," I replied. "But I really want the chance to make it for once."

Sadly, I did not make it into the play, and I had been heartbroken, moping for days on end, for everything I had worked so hard for was lost. My second semester was on a downer, as other girls in the drama club had continued to mock me for my appearance.

"Look at that peary girl," I once heard someone mock. "Thinks she looks like a fairy."

"Don't mind her," Roberta had said to me before I could break down. "All of them are just a bunch of losers. No need to step down to their level."

"Yeah, well those losers as you call them, they are just..."

"They are just so full of themselves because they get their way all the time. And that is what you will turn into if you got your way too."

I was aghast at her words. How could she say that about me?

"You know, we could do something better," she suggested. "Let us go ahead and make our own little movie. If you can't get in through the front door, try the back door."

I grinned at her line of thinking and pinched myself. Of course, I didn't have to just sit around and try and suck up to those in charge. I can go out and make something happen.

The next day, during lunch, she gathered her brother Brad and his best friend Kevin Wilson and sat them down.

"We are going to work on a movie this summer," Roberta had been saying. "I wanted to recruit you guys to help us out. Let's share some ideas and all, what do you say?"

"Sure thing," her brother replied. "What is the story going to be about?"

"We will do A Midsummer Nights' Dream," I said.

"Yeah, a modern-day retelling of the Shakespearean comedy," Roberta added. "I think it will be an awesome story."

"Sure sounds like it." That was from Kevin. "But I don't know if I want to act."

"Oh, come now," Roberta persuaded. "It will be fun."

"It is hard work, and I don't want to make a fool of myself," he replied. "I am a lousy actor."

"You are not, I saw your performance in the play," Roberta shot back.

"Yeah, come on Kevin," Brad replied. "We can do this one with the two lovely ladies."

I blushed at his remark.

Kevin thought about it for a while. "Very well. But let Dorothy here write the script. She is good at that task."

I grinned and agreed to the task, for it was indeed a dream coming true even as we spoke.

And so our project was underway. We spent the whole summer filming our story, about four lovers intertwined in the affairs of love and confused affections. In our version, I was Helena, a maid who had met and fallen in love with Demetrius (Kevin), a wealthy businessman, a la Cinderella. Only the "prince" then dumps her for Hermia (Roberta), a model who was already in love with her man, Lysander (Brad), a football player.

It was a funny story, this version. We had Demetrius, madly in love with Hermia, stooping low to get her, including trying to have Lysander framed for robbery or drug use. Helena, meanwhile, jealous for Demetrius' affections, attempts similar measures to spoil things for Hermia.

Things reached a climax when Demetrius succeeds in framing Lysander, who gets imprisoned and then hypnotized by a henchman. He meets Helena, who was cleaning the jails, and, falling madly in love with her due to the spell, breaks out of jail to pursue her. Hermia, meanwhile, uncovers Demetrius' scheme. He gets arrested on charges of stalking, while Lysander, still under the spell, is no longer interested in Hermia. Fortunately, things get sorted out in the end, and everyone lives happily ever after.

The whole time, I found that I really enjoyed this task, for I was now getting somewhere as an actress. I was starting to become somebody, anyone but the "loud pear" as everyone loved to call me.

After making our little movie, we managed to secure use of the school's auditorium to show it during afternoons. I made out some posters and with approval from our principal, posted them around the school.

Despite all our efforts, there were still a number of detractors amongst the kids. "You went and spoiled a longstanding Shakespearean classic?" I once heard one girl demand.

"Ugh, that pear is doing this movie. Must be a terrible one," another person remarked.

Before long, some of the more popular kids had begun boycotting the movie and harassing other kids not to go see it, all because I was involved in the film. Only a handful of students got to see the film, and those who did, they all enjoyed it, but that didn't help me feel better.

"Don't write them off," Roberta had said to me. "Those kids matter too. You are becoming just like those other bullies when you consider their opinions don't count."

"I know," I replied. "But after this, I just feel I won't make it as an actress."

"You cannot let that be the end," she went on. "I mean, someday, something just might open up, but you cannot just let life pass you by. If the back door is closed, then perhaps you ought to try something else."

Unable to say anything else, I only sighed as we made our way out. I was crushed to have been despised, even though I had given everything I had.

That changed the following day when I had a new surprise. I was called in to see Mr. Harding, Kevin's father and the faculty advisor of the school newspaper.

"Ms. Reagan," he had began, "I got to see you film a couple of times, and I think you have a future in television."

I blushed. "Thank you sir," I said. "Acting is my passion."

"That really is evident," he replied. "Well, I want to offer you a post here at the paper. We are opening a new televised portion to the school newspaper. We hope to film events, including games and other breaking stories, and then broadcasting those on our website as well as on the new television displays we are putting up throughout the campus. I wondered if you would be willing to head this up."

I pondered the offer for a moment, for it was a detour from acting, and I didn't have too much experience as a news reporter. But I figured that I could recruit other guys to help me out here. I agreed to the task, and before long, I was holding a new post.

It was in this role when I met Harry for the first time. He had come out to Chicago for a major high school basketball tournament which was hosted at our school, and featured some of the biggest high school stars around the nation.

An underage varsity player, Harry, was becoming widely known as a basketball phenomenon, billed to be the next Michael Jordan by some pundits. As such, I had been assigned to interview him before the game.

We arranged to have the interview up in our "news room," that is our main studio. Here it was a little bit quieter. We would have just over half an hour before he had to go downstairs to join the team to prepare for their game that evening.

I set up a couple of armchairs in front of a green screen, on which I would post images of different basketball logos. The rest of the crew worked quickly to have the equipment set up.

Harry came on in, dressed in his basketball gear. Upon seeing me, he stopped, somewhat embarrassed, wondering if he should have been more formally dressed for the interview, for I was wearing a two-piece suit and looking all business.

I laughed and beckoned him over. "Come on in," I said. "Have a seat, the outfit serves the purpose perfectly." I stood up and greeted him with a handshake and he smiled back at me.

He was a cute guy. Tall, blonde, and lean, he exuded a confident swagger. I was somewhat taken to him on that first meeting.

"It is nice to meet you," he replied. "So shall we begin to get the show on the road?"

As we sat down, I had the crew cue up our cameras and then I began asking him some questions.

"Tell us about yourself."

"How did you get to be a basketball player?"

"Who has been your main influence behind the sport?"

As I went over the questions, he gladly shared his stories, talking about his father and his influence in helping develop him as a player. He discussed all of the different things he had done as a child. By the time we were done, I felt we had a good story at hand. I smiled and thanked him for his time. "Good luck tonight," I said as I walked him to the door.

That evening, we were down at the gymnasium, where the game had been held, for we were also assigned to record and broadcast the game. The place had been filled to capacity, for there were many fans who were interested in seeing some of the up and coming players who were on tonight, especially Harry.

I had seen clips of the boy in action, and he was certainly a thrill to watch, as well as a natural heartthrob. He was graceful and swift in his move, and every time he got on the court, he seemed to take the game over by himself.

Everyone had stood at attention for the opening prayer and national anthem, and then the players took their places on the court for the initial toss-up. Right away, Harry had gone to work – his centerman caught the ball and passed it over to him, he rushed through the opponents and fired a shot so quick and seamless that everyone just stood by and watched as he sunk the ball.

He was certainly the real deal all right, for that evening, he continued to show his mettle, while the opponents, visibly flustered, looked ready to give up. They eventually tried to stop him, but nothing seemed to work, for he seemed to flow through everyone like water, and always had the ball in the net, whether it was a quick shot or a nice pass. By the end of the day, his team won with a score of 80-58, and he had scored a total of 42 points.

We had a story to tell. As we got back to the studios, I went over all the clips and began assembling our little news reel, and the guys even filmed a brief commentary on Harry.

"Ladies and gentlemen, Michael Jordan has been reborn and is ready to rock the world." That was from Brad, who served on the news team. He proceeded to deliver his opening comments, before turning over to Kevin, his partner on the set. They looked like professionals, all right, the way they carried on with their spiel.

From here on, I was beginning to feel confident that my efforts were paying off and I was beginning to get recognition for my work. With that, I began to make some more friends and was no longer the shunned pear, but a more popular girl.

Before long, the pear itself disappeared. I had more time to go work out and eventually lost the weight. By the end of the year, I had trimmed down my frame.

When I graduated, I was determined to make it into drama school and train to become a Broadway actress. Either that or I could go to film and television school and go into journalism.

Chapter 2

AFTER GRADUATING, I had gone and applied to several film and television schools across the country, but despite all my effort, I could not get into any of them, for admission to these schools had been really competitive.

I was disappointed, but unwilling to be discouraged, I instead enrolled in business school at UCLA, taking the marketing stream. It was a good fit, for I found that I really enjoyed the challenges of business and marketing, which played well to my creativity and enterprising nature.

My parents were proud of me, for no one in my family has ever made it to college. I was determined to make my mark and seize on whatever came along.

On arriving there, I soon learned that Harry's brother, Fred was also attending UCLA and was serving as student body president. I got first got to see him when he had given a welcome speech during our orientation session, and then came around to personally greet us after all the presentations.

"Hi," he had said, approaching me with a handshake. "I'm Fred. Welcome to UCLA."

"I'm Dorothy," I responded.

"Nice to meet you," he continued. "I recognize you. You interviewed my brother during that tournament a few years ago."

I beamed at him. "Wow, isn't it ever a small world," I gushed.

"Yeah, really," he went on. "What program are you doing here?"

"I am doing business. But I really wanted to go to film school; that was my passion."

"I see. Well I guess sometimes, life throws the detour in the way and all. I am doing law, but I really wanted to play professional basketball. Harry on the other hand, he was born to play. Our dad instilled the game in us, and he took it and really ran away." He paused, and then added, "I did get to watch that movie you did in high school."

I beamed yet again, and my eyes nearly bulged out of my head. "You got to see my film?" I exclaimed.

"Harry had been given a copy from someone up there. My word, we were laughing our guts out, it was totally funny." He chuckled and then added, "Yeah, it was a good film. You are a good actress."

We continued to talk for a while, before he gone and introduced me to all the different student services available. "Let us know if you ever need anything," he had said after we had finished. "We are here to serve the student body in any way possible."

That was the beginning of my freshman year. Toward the end of the year, I remembered that when word surfaced that Harry was bound to be coming here the following year, a buzz of excitement had swept through the campus. Realizing the hype surrounding him, I was quick to seize on it; choosing to make posters and T-shirts of him for a class assignment. But Fred had an even better idea.

"You could make a commercial," he suggested. "I have a lot of footage of him in action. Real good shots, can strike fear right into you like a bolt of lightning. Well, if you take the right clips and use effect."

I was intrigued. "I am a romantic," I replied. "I like that idea."

And so I set off with my project. I reviewed hours of footage with him, and in my mind, the picture was coming naturally to me. I picked out different sound tracks and other special effects, and before long, I had my advertisement ready to be presented.

My professor was so impressed when he saw the clip, he had gone and convinced the school to buy some airtime to show it on local television.

I began to receive more and more public acclaim for my work and before long, Fred approached me again, offering to have me oversee promotions for the student body for the coming year. I laughed and agreed to the task.

Harry arrived on the campus the following August on orientation day greeted with much fanfare the moment he arrived with his brother at the main entrance. Students were there waiting for him to arrive, asking for photographs and autographs.

That same day, while gathered out at the front entrance waiting for him, I had a surprise of my own when I was approached by Katie Kennedy, the head cheerleader at UCLA.

She was a gorgeous young woman, really trim with shiny brunette hair and brown eyes. And she had a vibrant, cheerful personality that really added life to a room. Right now, she was clad in her cheerleader's outfit, the blue figure-hugging dress with yellow trim, and white knee-length socks and sneakers. And she was talking to me.

"Dorothy," she had been saying, "I wondered if you would be interested in signing on to the cheerleading squad. You have that strong energy we need to get crowds going."

I laughed at first, very surprised at the invitation. Four years ago, I would not have made it onto the squad, for I had been overweight and not particularly attractive. I had managed to shed some pounds over the years.

"Why, of course, Katie. I would be glad to join you!" I exclaimed delightfully.

"Then, you are going to need these," Katie replied, handing me a set of pom-poms. "There's no time to change, because he is going to be arriving pretty soon...oh, oh I think they're coming now." She pointed to a car that was pulling up.

"Places everyone!" I called out. Everyone stepped aside on either direction of the path to form an aisle. I could see someone holding up a "welcome" poster.

The car came to a stop and Harry alighted. Immediately, the crowd gathered there raised a cheer, and he waved to us. Katie and I were waving our pom-poms, along with the rest of the cheerleaders who were present there. A number of them did their backflips across the path.

As the car moved onward, he came toward us, waving to everyone, shaking hands, and offering autographs.

When he came to me, I beamed delightfully. "You remember me, don't you?"

"Oh, yes," he replied. "You're that pretty girl that interviewed me a couple of years back. I didn't know you were coming here."

I blushed at his comment. "I know," I jabbered. "Small world isn't it? Didn't Fred talk to you about my being here?"

"No, he never mentioned that," he said. Looking me over, he chuckled and added, "And it looks like somebody didn't wear her costume."

I laughed with his remark, as I had been wearing jeans and a t-shirt. "I know," I responded. "I just got recruited onto the squad just five minutes ago."

"Well I think your hair should make up for it," he went on. "It is like a stream of fire."

I laughed yet again as he moved onward. I was giddy that he remembered me and was giving me attention.

The year seemed to have gone by quickly. I was very busy, having to keep up with all of my classes and then I had duties with making promotional posters and commercials. Come game time, I was on the court with the girls as we led the cheers. My schedule had kept me up around the clock – I scarcely had an idea of how involving college life could be.

During my downtime, I would see Harry on multiple occasions, mainly because we somehow kept running into each other, wherever we went, in the hallways, the library, the coffee shops and cafeteria. I can recall one instance when I had just finished my classes for the day and was passing through the café on my way back to my dorm room when I ran into him.

"Are you following me?" I asked sarcastically. "I keep running into you everywhere we go."

"That's funny," he said, "because I was going to ask that same question."

I laughed. "Well, don't great minds think alike? What are you up to now?"

"I had just finished practice, and now I was going to sit down and try doing some studies." He indicated his backpack filled with books.

"That's nice," I replied. "I was doing the same thing. Want to study together?" I indicated to the sofas there.

Harry plopped himself down onto the armchair, and I sat down on the sofa alongside him. "So how were things going in basketball today?" I asked as I drew out my books.

"Well frankly, I don't like to practice," he replied. "I am most happy during game time, when my mind can focus better and I know what I am doing. During practice sessions, things are somewhat staged and unnatural. It's on the court when somehow, everything comes to me and I can pick up the right moves."

"Cool stuff. Yeah, I am always taken with amazement whenever you take to the court and really blow past everyone. You can be a Hall of Fame player someday."

We sat and chatted for a while before finally getting down to work. As we sat there, he did ask me a couple of questions for some of the classes and I willingly helped him out.

We sat there right until dinner time and at his suggestion, we went out together to Planet Hollywood on Rodeo Drive.

I felt it was a splurge for a college student to be spending big dollars here, but Harry reassured me that he had money. "I had been teaching basketball to kids during the summer time," he was saying as we came inside.

"That sounds like fun," I replied.

"Yeah, so tell me, what were you going for after you graduate?"

"Well, I am doing a business major, in the marketing stream. Actually, I'm currently in charge of all the promotional stuff for the student body. I was in charge of all those posters and billboards that you see all around the campus.

"But my real dream had been acting. My mom was a small-time actress, appeared in a few plays back in Chicago. But her dream was to break into Hollywood, but she could never come close. I had done one movie, but I never could get into film school myself. So I'm doing business instead."

"I see," he responded. "So what do your folks do?"

"My father was a construction worker," I answered. "Mother a waitress. I am the only child in the family and the first person from the clan to go to college. Had received an academic scholarship and that's how I made it to UCLA."

"Wow. You are a driven person."

"Well, yeah I have a lot on my plate. I want to make something of myself, be someone."

I continued to pour out my inner feelings to him about life, and for a while, he sat there and listened, before the servers finally came along to take our orders.

After dinner, as we walked back to the campus, he indicated that he needed help with some of his classes. "I need to keep my grades to keep playing," he had said. "You've taken English Literature and American History. Wondered if you could help me with those classes."

I had so many things on my plate, but spending time with the boy? It's an opportunity not to pass up. "Sure, I could help you out, say once a week?" I replied.

And so we would meet up from then on every week, and I offered to help him with things. In return, he was willing to help me with designing my promotional posters and he even filmed some commercials, even those not related to basketball.

From time to time, I did join him in the gymnasium, playing a round of ball myself. I felt somewhat like a little girl following her older brother around and possibly slowing him down, but he didn't seem to care too much.

For us, it was the seeds beginning to sprout as we began hanging out more and more. We went out to dinner on a couple more occasions and attended a social function together. But we were not official yet, for he had been going out with other girls as well. I patiently sat back, aware that perhaps if we moved too quickly too soon, other girls would get jealous.

The year had gone flying by and before long, it was getting toward the end of April, and basketball season was winding down to a close. The UCLA Bruins had gone to the Final Four for the past five years, but they had not been successful in sealing that elusive national title. This year, everyone knew, was going to be different, now that we had the Molokai Express on board.

We swept through the playoffs with relative ease, sealing our usual spot in the Final Four. That was when the real trouble began to arise, when we faced the defending national champions, USC in the semi-finals. They were a seasoned team, and they were ready for a fight, for they knew they had to contend with Harry Madison.

I can still recall game day, there was buzz in the stadium, all filled to capacity with all the fans, eager to see the Southern California showdown and the new rising star. We performed our usual routine, dancing and flipping on the court, waving our pom-poms. The setting of the stage.

And from the word go, the game was on. USC had come out flying against us, and for a while, even Harry seemed up against a wall. They were doing an effective job, shutting him down, while they were flying in the opposite direction. By the end of the second half, we were down 50-15.

We were all stunned, but nobody gave up hope. As the teams made their way off to their locker rooms, we took to the court once more, carrying out our cheers and calling upon fans to make noise and encouraging them not to give up. Everyone raised their voices and got to their feet – it seemed the roof could blow off the top of the building.

As the teams came back out to the court, I remembered seeing Harry talking to some of his teammates. I could not make out what they were saying, but I remembered seeing the resolute look on his face as they took to the court once more.

"Come on, Harry," I said under my breath. "You got to pull this one through."

And he did, for next thing I realized, he had taken the ball, and gone flying through the opponents to swoop the ball into the net. Before long, he had found his groove, and the Bruins had indeed found theirs.

Both teams battled hard, but it was evident that we were catching up. The noise in the building grew louder and louder. The girls continued to wave the pom-poms, cheering on as the game drew to a close. Harry had just managed to net a basket to take the lead for the first time, as we drew into the final minute of play, up 82-81. USC continued to battle out, but then, Harry's brother Fred sunk a three-pointer to build on the lead. Our defense managed to hold out and eventually the game was over and we emerged victorious.

It was not over yet, for we then had to play Duke University for the national title. It was a grueling game, but similar to USC, we battled back from an early-game deficit as Harry soon took the whole game over in the waning minutes to help lock up the victory.

Pandemonium swept through the building, for we seemed to have accomplished the impossible, taking down the defending champions, and having to battle back from an early-game deficit. Celebrations ensued, lasting all night, and I'm sure nobody got any sleep on campus.

Preparations for final exams were challenging, for I had put off a lot of study time to fit things in. But by now, I was riding on so much energy, I managed to sail through my exams and receive top marks.

Chapter 3

THE YEARS HAD COME and gone and by the time I graduated, I had been hired as an assistant PR coordinator by Tom Adams, a Hollywood producer and the new owner of the Los Angeles Clippers, the team that had drafted Harry two years ago. My role was to help oversee marketing and public relations of his entertainment properties. This role would see me working alongside several big name celebrities, both actors and basketball players with the focus on boosting their profile.

I was thrilled to land this job, for as far as I was concerned, I had made it. I had gone farther than my parents, having graduated from college and held a good job, with promise to go further.

Not long afterward, he received the news he had been looking forward to: Harry Madison finally agreed to play and signed on to the team. For two years, he had remained at UCLA and seemed somewhat reluctant to join the Clippers, given their consistent losing history, something that Adams was set on reversing, and that was one of my biggest challenges at hand on the job.

I had met with Harry just before training camp. He was surprised to see me with the organization.

"It looks like we are ending up in the same place at the same time, everywhere we go," he remarked. "I never expected to see you here."

I smiled at him. "Isn't this a small world?"

We had gone out for coffee at a small shop just across from Staples Arena. More than just a regular date, I was to work with him to help raise his profile. We managed to sell some tickets to people at the store and he gave out autographs to some fans.

"It sure looks like we have quite a task at hand," I had said, reflecting on the reception the team had been getting from the fans. "It is going to be a tough draw, trying to compete with the Lakers, especially given this team's dismal history and all. It's funny too, how some people are already taking bets on how long you will stay here, given their history as a revolving door of talent."

Harry chuckled a little. "I know what they mean," he replied. "But I'm not here to give up trying. You can't go anywhere if you let your circumstances shipwreck you and tie you down."

I grinned yet again. He was determined to live up to the challenge, which should help make my job easier. "I'm glad you see things that way. And that's why I'm here, to help you go forth."

Harry appeared in a press conference shortly after training camp just days before the first game of the season. Having gone over with him things he ought to talk about to the press, he had followed some of my cues, concluding his statement with the bold declaration, "Read my lips, we will win the championship."

His comments had lit a firestorm that raged on nationwide. They appeared on the cover page of numerous magazines nationwide. Sports commentators were talking about him for weeks on end. "How could he make such an outrageous statement?" most of them had raged, for the Clippers were not even expected to make the playoffs that season, and given their history, a championship season seemed far-fetched even on the long-run. A few pundits expected he would be traded for established veteran players.

Harry later clarified his statements, saying that he would lead them to a championship before his three-year rookie contract expired, but he was adamant that they'd make the playoffs that season.

Regardless of our season's outcome, Harry's words helped achieve our first objective, to draw attention. Season ticket sales had risen considerably from last year, but Harry still had his game on the line – the time was coming to determine if he was the real thing or would fizzle out in classic Clipper style. I knew however that deep down inside, he was determined to make things happen.

From the opening toss-up, the Lakers were quick to jump all over the Clippers. Everything seemed futile as they racked up points to take a big lead by the end of the first half. But Harry rallied his teammates together at the start of the third quarter, and somehow mounted a comeback to eventually tie the game by the end of the fourth quarter and then seal a win in overtime on a last second cross-court shot Harry made.

The press was quick to seize on this epic first game, and many pundits were lauding Harry for Rookie of the Year honours. It was evident that he was the real thing, but we were aware there was more work to be done, and I was in on it with him.

About a quarter way through the season, I had gotten him involved in perhaps one of our most significant public relations efforts yet, when I approached the new principal of an inner-city high school in Eastern Los Angeles. It was a school that had a negative reputation in its community – academically, their students were performing poorly, graduation rates were low, and discipline was non-existent. The newly hired principal was determined to turn things around.

Having read in the local newspaper about the principal and his new pledge to improve conditions for his school, I phoned him up one afternoon and asked if I could come see him. Agreeing to the meeting, he came over to our offices promptly.

"I can see that you want to change things in your school," I had said to him after he had arrived. "I'm wondering what we can do to help you out."

We were up in my office, meeting over a cup of coffee.

"Well I am rather relieved that you are interested in helping us," the principal had begun. "It is nothing short of an answered prayer."

"At the heart of the matter," he continued, "our school is really lacking in purpose. We have hired new teachers and are making an effort to improve discipline. But I want to help our students come out and find some purpose before they start killing themselves socially, or even literally, given their self-destructive mindset."

"Okay, well do you guys have a basketball team?"

"We do. And there are guys who like to go out and play."

I smiled. "Well, we are in the basketball business. I'm wondering if we could volunteer one of our players to run an after-school program."

After the meeting, I called up Harry and asked him if he would be interested in doing the after-school program with the kids.

"Surely, you can't be serious," was his first response.

"Oh, I'm serious," I replied. "It is all about public image."

"Come on now," he went on, "I already have..."

"Now Harry, what do you really have going outside of game time and practicing basketball?" I interrupted. "Do you want to just go on wasting your time twiddling your thumbs between games or do you want to be actively involved in helping change someone's life?"

With some prodding, I managed to get him to agree to participate. Every Thursday or Friday, depending on his game schedule, unless he was away on a road trip, he would come over to the school and teach skills to the kids in school. The students were slow to pick up on his lessons, but they were inspired to be in the presence of an up-and-coming NBA star.

Word quickly got around of his involvement with the program. Several reporters had shown up to the school to interview him about things. The positive attention proved beneficial to boost his image as well as that of the team. Ticket sales continued to climb as the Clippers billed themselves as a franchise that reaches out to the community.

Not long afterward, I then persuaded actress Heidi Polk who'd signed onto a contract with Mr. Adams' film productions to participate as a drama teacher. We had just released a movie starring her, and I anticipated her subsequent participation in the program could boost our box-office. Since I had experience as a director, I volunteered to help her run the program. We were right yet again, as her involvement helped raise her profile.

And before long, that school managed to achieve its mission, for their students were beginning to find their own personal mission. Test scores and literacy rates were rising, their basketball team was winning games, and they even developed a quality drama program. Our success was so evident, we soon moved out from that school and launched our own after-school basketball and drama academy, volunteering several more of our entertainers on contract.

As our organization gained recognition, we soon began cross marketing our movies with the Clippers. Several actresses had joined the team's cheerleading squad, and that helped to draw in more basketball fans. In return, a number of Clipper players had played bit roles in some of our films.

Harry was one of several players to have held bit roles. Halfway through the season, he had played a henchman for a Mexican drug lord who had been on the run from the police. Having been present on the set, I was surprised by his acting skill, for he seemed to quickly pick up on his role and become the character.

He had emerged from hiding behind a set of barrels, loading his gun, looking as though he were ready to go and kill somebody. I can still see those intense eyes that could put the fear of lightning into you as he looked about grimly, gun barrel ready. He soon emerged, hopped on a motorcycle and rode off. On the very next shot, he had stashed his package of drugs in hiding, and then whipping out his mobile phone, he made a call.

"The package has been delivered," he had said, his voice gravelly, rough. "Right at the point where you asked me to..."

He continued on with his dialogue, which ultimately ended in him threatening to kill his boss if he didn't get paid. He only appeared in a few more scenes, and his character would wind up being killed.

I really didn't like this movie, naturally, because I was especially sensitive about Harry's image. He was supposed to be a good guy after all. But he didn't mind. "I had a lot of fun doing this," he had said when we had met once, briefly. "I used to do theatre as a kid, along with playing basketball."

"Yeah, I'm just a little bit conscientious about your image," I replied. "I mean, the Clippers' star player being such a thug, it's not really fitting."

"Well, I know what you mean," he responded. "But I have no regrets. It's probably going to give the fans a little laugh."

"That's for sure. Well you really scared the living daylights out of me."

He chuckled. "Well I guess then nobody could then believe it was I who was the henchman."

The movie was released just before the playoffs began. Even though Harry had only four or five scenes in the whole movie, we decided to derive portions of those scenes to make a commercial billing our quest to go the distance in the playoffs. It would start with Harry drawing his gun and making a daring threat in a showdown, before cutting swiftly to his game time action.

This commercial would prove to be a big hit, and would help to promote the movie as well as the games. We soon began offering fans free movie tickets to this show along with basketball admissions.

On the court, Harry had succeeded in leading the Clippers to the playoffs as we finished with a healthy 45-37 record, easily their best record in a decade. We had lost in the first round, going 2-4 against the Los Angeles Lakers, but at least we had the initial breakthrough to give us some credibility.

As he grew in recognition, there were marketers eager to approach him for endorsements. That's where I came in, working alongside his agent Fred, we worked out endorsement contracts with numerous companies, most notably Nike, who launched a line of shoes and athletic wear under the Molokai Express label.

Following his second season, at my suggestion, he had launched a sports bar under the Harry's name, which we owned together, along with several other investors. It proved to be a popular joint, and by the time the following season began, we had opened restaurants in five different locations around Los Angeles.

Chapter 4

WE WERE A BIG HAPPY family, and it was not long before a number of relationships emerged between our basketball players and actors. By springtime, there had been three weddings held.

Naturally, these relationships had garnered much public attention and the press was quick to seize on speculations on the couples and their private lives. Magazines often carry gossip about the big stars of the day, and the more a star tries to hide away in their private life, the more relentless they get in pursuing them and speculating into the person's private life.

But this is where my job had come to play. As an assistant PR coordinator, I often served as an advisor, working alongside their agents to help protect the celebrities from damaging revelations and help build their image. Starting the previous year, I had already gotten the stars involved in different community activities and encouraged them to open up their private lives a little more.

"Being a movie star with a number of fans is like having several more friends," I had explained. "How would you like it if your friends never came to see you or showed interest in you? That's what it's like with stars that remain distant and aloof, people want to stick their noses in their private lives and could soon make assumptions and inferences that aren't necessarily true. You got to give even more of yourselves when they stick their noses in further."

One couple had gone down to Mexico to help with a construction project. Another couple had volunteered at a therapeutic center for drug users.

Even if some people don't get involved in volunteering public time, most stars would often speak openly about their own lives. Some people invited the press into their own homes, but most of the time, they would openly greet and interact with people on the streets, handing out autographs openly. These tactics indeed helped deflect a lot of negative rumours that often pervaded most stars, and in so doing, they helped build a more positive, personal image with the public. And when I talked to some of them, they seemed to have a much happier, healthier private and public life.

It was not all rosy and perfect, for there were several relationships that ended in a rather messy separation, which drew negative attention from the press. I was frustrated, watching this unfold, but I realized that not everyone was perfect, sometimes relationships hit the rocks. Fortunately, nobody sustained damage to their image, and they continued to carry on with life.

Of all our stars, basketball players or actors, nobody drew a bigger following than Harry, who was a social butterfly. He had dated numerous actresses and models from his first year of professional basketball. Halfway through his third year, he did get married to one actress, Kristen Jackson. It seemed like a match made in heaven, at least to those on the outside, but things ended in a messy divorce in May, right in the middle of the playoffs.

It was not a pretty affair, for there was a lot of backbiting between the two. She posed fairly hefty demands, while he insisted that she had cheated on him. Court battles soon ensued.

Meanwhile, we were concerned that Harry would meltdown on the basketball court amidst this personal battle. That has always been the Clippers' history, their stars somehow melt down just as they are about to get somewhere. The press has been quick to speculate on how he would be able to handle the meltdown and many believed the team would be defeated soundly.

However, despite the detractions, Harry seemed not to be affected, for he continued to press on, eventually leading them past the Lakers in the semi-finals and then taking down the defending champions Boston Celtics to seal the first championship for the Clippers.

The whole basketball world had been stunned by this turn of events. But it served well to help build him into a basketball legend, someone who was able to conquer the impossible: remain unaffected by a messy divorce and come away with a seemingly impossible victory on a team that nobody thought could ever win. As a result, one magazine had billed Harry as the "Teflon Express."

I recalled meeting up with him that summer, following the final game. We were down at the studios, doing a promotional photo shoot. There, he began to open up to me.

"You had taken quite a beating this spring," I had remarked once, while we were out for a date that summer. "Who could have endured as much as you have?"

He somehow managed a smile. "Yeah," he replied. "Actually, from the get go, right after our first night, things weren't good. In a way, it's a relief, but things could have been worse. I just sat back and waited for her to blink first and go have an affair. It would give me a good excuse to file for divorce. She is a loser."

I looked at him, partially shocked at his carefree attitude toward her, but I didn't know how to respond to that.

The court battles continued to rage on that summer, with both sides presenting strong cases against each other. Fortunately, there wasn't much damage to their public image – they remained popular with their fans at large. Still, the backbiting made me sick, and I personally wanted to pull Harry out of it.

An opportunity would open up when Mr. Adams had called me into his office one morning, just a week later. "I got to see your little movie you did in high school," he had said. "Harry showed me the video last night when he had come over for dinner."

I beamed. "Wow, and what did you think?"

"I thought it was a shame you didn't make it into film school. I know they are quite selective and all, but..." He then reached over and gripped my hands. "Some people don't need to go to school," he concluded.

I smiled, but not knowing what to say, I let him continue.

"Well that's the long speech," he chuckled. "In short, I think I would like to have this movie filmed."

Now I was really beaming from ear to ear. "I would love that," I replied. "Under one condition though: I want to star in the movie."

"That can be done," he replied. "There are some things you'll need to work on before acting, but I can arrange for you to learn what you need to know."

And so we were off to the races. I had taken some acting lessons and before long, I had smoothened over my rough spots. Meanwhile, the directors consulted me on how I wanted the details of the movie to turn out.

I soon persuaded Harry to star in the movie. "It's a great way to raise your profile," I said while we were out at his new sports bar down in Malibu. "And you did do some acting in high school. You should star in it with me."

Harry grinned. "Well, I can give this one a try," he replied.

"Yeah, well you already have quite a profile on your plate. Your face appears on so many magazines across the country, it is marketed in many different consumer products, and you even appeared in one movie. Now we run a sports bar with your own name. Starring in a movie should add fuel to the fire."

Having agreed to appear in the movie, we only needed to cast two other roles. Those roles went to veteran actors Joan Ford and Casey Grant, who would be cast as Helena and Demetrius respectively, while Harry and I would be Lysander and Hermia.

Because filming the movie overlapped with Harry's basketball schedule, we had to coordinate our schedule accordingly, often filming between games and during a Clippers home stand, when

he was around to film. We mostly used the soundstage and a few
on-location scenes around the city.

It was my dream coming true, all right, for now I was beginning
to break through as an actress. I can recall every moment of every
shoot, from the opening scene – with Harry and I on a date,
interrupted when we ran into Casey, who tried to woo me away – to
the closing scenes when Harry and I kissed.

It was then when I realized that Harry and I were meant to be
together, but I didn't know if he shared the same thoughts. But I
decided to seize on things one day when we were together on a date
while skiing up at Lake Tahoe, the day before the premiere of our
movie.

The snow was fresh and powdery as we took to the hills, flying
down the runs, an ideal day to go skiing. There were numerous other
skiers present and a few of them recognized Harry and waved to him
as they passed us by.

I was laughing away as I glided downhill, often trying to racing
Harry. He was much more experienced than I was, so I could never
catch him.

At one point, when we were riding up on the gondola together, I
decided to kick up a conversation.

"Doesn't it feel like a small world?" I had begun when we came
in from the surf. "Somehow, we always wind up in the same place at
the same time. The first meeting in high school, then we attend the
same college, and here we are today."

He smiled and reaching out, he gripped me by the shoulders
and I took note of a gleam in his eye. "It is quite a coincidence," he
remarked.

"I think it is about fate," I continued. "Don't you think it means
something?"

His smile turned to a muse as he gripped his chin in thought, but
he didn't say anything at first.

"Come now," I continued. "Who was there, when you needed her most? You know the answer."

By now, we were at the top of the hill, and as we exited the lift, he smiled yet again, and gripped my shoulder. "Girl, we are just friends, you know," he said. I began to frown at which, he went on, "Oh, Dorothy that isn't such a bad thing?"

Tears began to form at my eyes. "Is this the thanks I get?" I cried. "I mean, after..."

He interrupted me by pulling me close and kissing me, but I knew he was disingenuous. As soon as he let go of me, I turned and slapped him across the face, before turning and running toward the snow. I could hear him coming after me.

"Dorothy!" he called out. "Girl, I'm sorry, I didn't mean to..."

I interrupted him with a laugh, and turning back to him, I fluttered my eyes as I stepped into my skis. "I bet you can't catch me!" I yelled back. I pushed off downhill and began racing down the run again. Before I could get far, he skittered ahead of me, laughing away.

"I got you all right," he shouted with a laugh and I continued to chase after him as we sailed away once more.

The premiere was held the following day down at the Chinatown Theatre. I remembered riding in a limousine down to Chinatown for our premiere. As we came to a stop in front of the theatre, I alighted first to a large applause and a sea of flashing cameras. I smiled and waved.

Just then, I noticed a familiar face in the crowd. Kevin Harding was standing right behind a line, microphone and paper pad in hand. A cameraman stood behind him.

"Kevin!" I beamed. "I didn't realize you were now on the press."

"Sure thing," he replied, turning back to the camera, he continued, "And here is Dorothy, the star of the film. A relatively new face on Hollywood and someone who looks to emerge as a rising star."

He pulled the microphone in front of me, but not knowing exactly what to say, I smiled, waved at the camera and then said, "Nice to see my old friend again." I then moved onward, joined by the rest of my co-stars as we made our way inside.

As we came inside, I saw, standing with the directors, Roberta, my old friend from high school. She smiled and reached over to hug me.

"I hope you haven't forgotten me, now that you are famous," she joked.

I laughed ironically. "You will get your cut of the profits," I replied. "You should be in Hollywood yourself."

She smiled again. "Thanks. I'm actually in New York, on Broadway. I can't believe you didn't try and get me to star in this film. How could you do that to your best friend?"

"Oh, I'm sorry, but I didn't have your phone number. But next time, we can film something together, perhaps."

We made our way inside and before long the showing was underway, open to the press for the first time. I could sense the room was really engaged, following the movie closely. I smiled, realizing that indeed this movie could be my big break, a dream that had found me when I had given up on it.

Just then, I saw Harry offering me his handkerchief, and I didn't realize that I had been tearing up. I accepted it gratefully and wiped my face. He then reached over and gripped my hands and smiled at me.

I was moved to see the whole movie come together like this. It was indeed a very humorous recreation of the classical Shakespeare, appropriately done. I could only imagine now how much this show would do at the box office.

When the movie came to an end, I was ushered to the front of the stage, along with the rest of my co-stars. The audience offered a large applause. I smiled and waved back at them. Once at the front of the room, they ushered me over to the microphone, and I gave my short speech.

"Thank you all," I began. "This is a dream come true...to..." For a moment, I lost my train of thought, and feared I could choke up on my big moment.

"To make a nice spin on my favourite play," I said. "I believe my fellow collaborators are here in the room tonight. We did this in high school and had a lot of fun doing so. It was a privilege to let you all see it tonight."

I called for my friends to stand up, and before long, cameras turned to get their pictures as well. I smiled and gave a few more words, before the ceremonies concluded.

After the show, I found Roberta in the crowd and went out with her for a little girl date. We went out to a coffee shop in Beverly Hills, not too far from my flat.

"Well, you sure made it," she had been saying when we were seated. "How does it feel?"

"I am feeling on top of the world," I replied. "It feels great to have made it now."

"I'm sure it does. But I got to warn you, it doesn't get much easier from this point onward, because public life is very demanding. They can ask a lot from you, make you do things just to keep your image."

"Robbie, I work in PR. I know all about that. But I'm glad just to have this chance."

"Oh, I know what you are saying," she went on. "I'm just advising you to pursue this as a hobby, not a career. That's what I'm doing right now, while on Broadway. I find I won't get satisfaction if I tried to pursue it as a long-term career. My identity was never wrapped in this."

I looked at her, perplexed. Identity, I heard her use that word before, and how avoiding making drama life my identity should be the secret to my success. For goodness sake, she was always the most popular girl in school and had everything going for her, yet still went out of her way to befriend me.

Feeling uncomfortable, I changed the subject. "What do you think about Harry?" I asked.

"Well what do you mean? I mean, he is quite an athlete, a fun guy..."

"I mean, well..."

Roberta somehow read my mind. "Oh, no, you are not falling for him, are you?" she said. "Dolly, now talk about someone who wraps his identity in his game and is painfully shallow..."

"I know all that," I interrupted, "but somehow, I think fate is leading us together." I proceeded to tell her about how we wound up in UCLA at the same time, and how I had been instrumental in helping launch him as a star.

"But most importantly," I concluded, "he needs someone, and I understand him, not like those other stars whom he's been chasing after. I got to make him see that he belongs with me."

"Well, do you really understand him?" Roberta challenged. "He doesn't take women seriously."

"I know, but I can change him," I responded. "I'll show you."

Roberta seemed to have given up trying to refute me. "Okay, well if you say so," she concluded. "Well, let's move on and talk about happier things, shall we?"

We spent another hour, continuing to catch up as friends before I retired back to my home, now determined more than ever to make him mine.

Chapter 5

THREE YEARS HAD GONE by. Our movie had scored big in the box office, leaving me flush with cash and initially brimming with hope for my career as an actress, but after starring in two more movies that only flopped I soon found I wasn't taking off as full-fledged star in the long run.

So instead, I decided I would go into business for myself, running an advertising agency. I was extraordinarily busy, working very long hours for the first month. I eventually built a good team of marketers and creative directors and before long, we were well underway.

Meanwhile, Harry and I have been dating for quite some time, though he continued to see other girls. That gradually began to change, and he gradually began to see the light.

Today, Harry and I were down at the beachfront this time surfing, just off of Malibu. It was a beautiful spring afternoon by the beachside. The sun was scorching and the waves were breaking strongly toward the beachfront. It was an ideal day to go surfing.

I can recall as we came in from the surf and he came and pulled me aside, underneath a palm tree.

"Dolly," he began, "I need to apologize to you for being so ignorant over the past couple of months. I really shouldn't have given you a brush off so soon."

I smiled at him, but let him carry on.

"Well, I could tell that you wanted to be more than friends," he went on. "But... at that point, I wasn't ready to commit to anyone again. I thought I would just keep the company of a number of female friends for that time. You know?"

My smile faded a little. "I know," I replied. "But I'm surprised, because I thought you said you didn't get affected by a breakup."

"Well, truth is I realized I have my own personal limits," he replied. "And I got to smarten up and settle down with one person, instead of chasing after the wind. And well, we are but friends, but well you have played an important role in getting me to this point."

I blushed a little. "Say no more," I interrupted him. "You are going to ask me to marry you."

This time, it was his turn to blush, and for a moment, he was tongue-tied. I merely smiled and went on.

"My answer Harry Madison is yes," I concluded. "I can see that we do have a future together and I want to seize that."

He blushed again. "No, that was not what I was going to say," he responded, but I could detect some hesitation in his voice.

I grinned at him once more. "Oh really," I replied. "Don't try and deny the truth." Turning and grabbing my board, I looked back at him with a wink. "Catch me if you can," I added and ran back toward the water.

I did not get far, for he caught up to me and grabbed me by the arm. I squealed and dropped my board, and he spun me around and before I knew it, he had swept me off my feet and holding me in a single arm, he pulled me close to him.

"Dolly, you aren't trying to run from me, are you?" he asked sarcastically and I giggled. Pulling me close, he kissed me again and this time I could tell he was genuine.

That evening, I was bragging to Roberta over the phone. "Girl, didn't I tell you I would get him? Well I did!" I had been exclaiming.

"That's unbelievable," she replied. "Well congratulations and I hope that you don't get caught..."

"Hey, that's not going to happen," I insisted. "Not after getting the guy like this."

"Well, if you say so," she responded. "Oh, speaking of which, Kevin and I just got engaged."

"Oh, really?"

"Yeah, we were on a date just the other day, and he proposed to me. We are planning our marriage just two weeks before Christmas, here in New York."

I was smiling so hard, a teardrop fell from my eye. "Robbie, I am so happy for you. I will be right there at your wedding."

"Uh, uh," she responded. "You are going to be my maid of honour."

That summer, to my dismay, and that of basketball fans nationwide, he chose to sign with the Heat that offseason, and Clippers' management didn't have the cap space to match the offer. Naturally, there was an uproar over the whole matter, and he was burned in effigy by many fans in California. I knew that he had done this largely to try and generate attention, to create a flair for the dramatic and stir some controversy.

I was unable to move with him to Florida right away, for my advertising business was still in its early stages, and I had tight deadlines to meet. I had been in and out of my office, meeting up with more clients and reviewing more reports. I eventually hoped to move the company to Florida in a year, once we had expanded.

The months had flown right on by. Just before Christmas time, I had to attend my friend's wedding up in New York City. Harry wasn't able to make it, for his team had been on a road trip, and he couldn't take time off, so I had let him off that time.

I can remember that day. I was taking it all in trying to imagine my own wedding. There was snow falling, and so we were bundled in warm overcoats over our dresses. As we rode to the cathedral in a limousine, I was looking outside at the fresh crisp snow falling on the ground. There were Christmas decorations on the street lights and windows on the store fronts. People were bustling about, getting things ready for Christmas.

Of course, my own wedding was in the springtime, so we wouldn't have any snowfall. But I still was getting an idea of what it would be like.

"You are rather quiet today," Roberta's words interrupted my thoughts. I looked up at her startled.

"Oh. Yeah, well I was just lost in thought."

"Yes, I can tell."

"I was thinking ahead to what my own wedding would be like and all." I sighed and added, "And it seemed like it was only yesterday we were children." A teardrop formed at my eye and I took a handkerchief and wiped it away.

"So much has happened," Roberta had agreed. "I never would have thought in my wildest dream that Kevin and I would be married. We were just a couple of childhood friends."

"I think it is a Midsummer Night's Dream affect," I replied, jokingly. "Well, more like mid-winter." She laughed at my remark.

Just then, we had pulled up to the cathedral in Lower Manhattan. As we made our way inside, an attendant took my winter coat before I filed on into the sanctuary in my new dress. I took in all the people in attendance, the ornately decorated walls and ceilings. I made my way forward, and stood to the side of the altar, just before Roberta entered in.

Everyone stood at attention and looked on at her, dressed in her flowing white gown. She smiled and filed forth accompanied by her father. The minister asked everyone to be seated.

The minister continued to proceed with the ceremony. I hung upon every word that happened until the very end when they were pronounced husband and wife and we proceeded out of the building.

"Don't forget about me, now that you are married," I had told Roberta jokingly as she and Kevin boarded their limo to head off to their honeymoon.

I spent Christmas with Harry down in Florida and for the first time, I had gotten to see the house he had bought, a three-story house overlooking the beachfront, with a swimming pool and basketball court in the backyard. It was a beautiful house, but it had become too much of a man's cave, with basketballs, weights, billiard tables, and televisions all over the place. The worst part, it reeked with sweat and beer.

I set about making the place my home. I imported some tapestries and had some of the rooms re-painted, and began cleaning out the smelly items, putting in air fresheners. The day after Christmas, I went out and bought some new furniture and re-designed the living room. I wanted to help insert my touch to the house before I moved in for good. Harry didn't feel comfortable with many of my changes, but I understood that he had designed according to his preference, which would have to change once I moved in.

I flew back to California, riding high with excitement, for everything had been falling into place. While in Florida, I had made contacts with several more businesses in the area, and things were falling into place for my relocation.

However, everything came crashing down one morning, just two weeks before our wedding. As I arrived at the office, I saw on a magazine cover a picture of Harry with Cherrie Lopez-Harrison. I picked up the magazine, staring at it in disbelief. For a moment, I had hoped that it was just a photo-op, but my gut told me that he had indeed gone and made out with another girl.

My face became flushed red with intense anger. I flung the magazine out into the trash bin and kicked it hard. Grabbing the phone, I called up Harry, determined to get to the bottom of this matter.

"Hello?" I could hear his voice on the other end. Inside, I forced myself to keep an even temper.

"Harry, do you have something to tell me?"

"Dolly, hey. I guess you saw the magazine."

"I did. Now what does this mean?"

"Oh, I will tell you what it means," he began, but I could hear some hesitancy in his voice. My ear perked up for whatever story he would cook up. "I was very drunk and then, next thing I knew..."

"Yes, you were kissing Cherrie Lopez-Harrison. Now is this the way that you treat me?"

"No, I..."

That was when my temper really boiled over. "You low down piece of slime!" I exploded. "Yes, you would very much rather have her wouldn't you? Wouldn't you?!" I could feel my face flushing red with anger.

"So you think that now is a perfect time to move on," I went on. "Oh, looky, here's a bigger fish. Well, if that is the way you want it, well then don't think you've seen the last of me. I will make you pay dearly for what you have done!"

With that, I slammed down the phone, ripping it from my desk, I proceeded to stomp it until it broke before smashing it through the window.

I then slunk down into my chair and sobbed. By now, I was simply overcome with anger and disbelief, for right when I thought I had my man, he had turned traitor on me.

It all came back to haunt me. Being turned down for a leading role in the high school play, not making it into film and television school, and now I was stuck in second fiddle marketing somebody else. And now, I had been deserted by my man. Everything was against me.

I burned in resentment towards everyone now. Old anger and hatred came flying back. I resented the kids who had taunted me in high school. I resented the high school drama directors who had passed me over for better looking actresses. I resented my own body, and began to wish that I was slimmer and had prettier hair. In short, I resented life itself, for now I had been chewed and torn asunder, and that is why to this day, I say that I don't get no satisfaction.

Interlogue

AS DOROTHY FINISHED her statement, the whole room was in shock at the whole turn of revelations. First, a celebrity marriage they never knew of. And now, the accusing party had been accused of breach of marital engagement. The press would have a mounting story that would be discussed for years and one could only speculate on the settlements the different parties could hope for.

Cameras were flashing and reporters were scrambling as Dorothy, tearing up dramatically, stepped down from the stand and, approaching Harry at the prosecutor's table, she slapped him hard. Before she could proceed further with her spat, deputies moved in to break up the fight.

At that point, Counsellor Bush called for Cherrie to take the stand. Cameras were flashing rapidly as the famous supermodel came out before the audience. Members in the audience excitedly pointed her out.

The young woman could stop a room with her appearance. She had a very slender figure with light brown, almost blonde hair, neatly arranged. Countless dimples accented her face. Her honey-brown eyes illuminated her face. Right now, they were grim with fear and a hint of uncertainty.

"Do you swear to tell the truth, the whole truth and nothing but the truth?" the bailiff asked.

"I do."

"Mrs. Madison," Bush began, "tell the court about your relationship in the affair."

Cherrie`s Story: Chapter 1

IT IS NOT EASY BEING me. I live a life that had been written out before I was ever born and like an actor cast for a role. I am a girl lost in the clamouring of life, bombarded on all sides and, unable to make a straight course for my life, others had decided for me where I was going in life and what I will do.

I was born out of wedlock to Marie Lopez-Harrison. A fashion student who worked in a South Carolina textile factory, she had a relationship with a NASCAR driver, my father. Their relationship had ended shortly before I was born, when he refused to help raise me.

Not long after that, the factory had closed down when the company outsourced labour overseas. Unemployed, she had moved to Michigan and found employment in Ford's Dearborn assembly line. In time, she had been taken in by Ted's parents, Gabriel and Michelle Lincoln, now respectively the CEO and executive vice-president of the company. They treated her as though she were their own daughter, as she had been long estranged from her parents.

My mother had big dreams for both of us. On top of working at the assembly line, she took evening classes to continue her fashion studies. She spent long hours in her little design studio, designing, sewing, and weaving.

At her persuasion, I began to participate as a model in junior pageants. It was something I enjoyed, for I loved fashions and colours. I loved helping her pick out different designs and then when I got onstage, the clothes became me as I would glide out onstage, presenting my wear, before doing my own optional performance, dancing a ballet or playing a piano piece. Once I recited poetry.

I can still recall participating in my International Junior Miss, wearing a frilly white dress that she had made. Gliding onto the stage I immediately sought out mommy and found her in the large audience, along with Ted and his family. At that moment, they were the only ones in the room with me as I carried out my routine, doing a ballet dance. As the music began to play, I closed my eyes, taking it all in, before I began, jumping and spinning, gliding across the stage, oblivious to others in the room.

After the final assessments, I was deemed the winner for my age group. I remember being greeted by a mass of cameras and a standing ovation. I was too shy to acknowledge the crowd applauding me; I just stood nervously as a judge set a crown on my head, and then gave a small wave to the applauding audience.

I remember mommy coming backstage after the show. Swooping me up, she kissed me on the cheek and I felt the tears streaming from her face.

"I'm so proud of you, baby," she was saying. "You did it. You did it for all of us."

Despite this success, I had been without a foundation. Growing up without a real father left a sore void in my life, for there was no one there to love me and guide me when I needed it most. I had grown terribly insecure when everyone began making big thing of me. While I loved modeling and performing for the heck of it, I began to feel exposed while under the public spotlight and often sought some refuge to hide. At school, I had been bullied by other kids who had grown jealous of all the attention I had been garnering, and that made me so insecure, I almost wanted to quit modelling, but I didn't have the courage to tell my mother about it.

At age 9, I had been sexually molested by a teacher, without a doubt, the most tormenting moment in my life. It left me with a general distrust for men and I was constantly on the lookout, wary of someone who wanted to take advantage of me.

I did not know how to cope with the pressure of being me. I had tried burying myself deeper into modelling, alternately coming out and flirting with the crowd one moment and then turning and withdrawing from them the next.

My relationships with other men followed the same pattern. Because I often found myself needing someone to lean upon, I would accept a date from a guy, but every time, I would begin to feel uncomfortable with him and not continue the date.

It was no surprise therefore that I accepted Ted's proposal, which was a breath of relief, for he was the only man I felt I could really trust in. Trouble is we lived in Florida, while he was away in Michigan, Virginia, or wherever they'd send him, and thus he never could always be there when I needed him most.

Deep inside, I did harbour feelings for him, after all we had been through together. However, I never told anyone about it, nor had I tried to pursue getting into a relationship with him, for he seemed content to be single and independent, and I was so afraid of being let down if he didn't have the same feelings. After all, we were simply friends or adopted siblings.

I remember that eventful date like it was yesterday; my mom and I were down in her design studio at home, designing and sewing some new clothing when the doorbell rang. When I got up to answer the door, there stood Tammy, his sister. Surprised, I reached out and greeted her with a hug. "Tammy!" I said. "Hey I was not expecting you today."

"How are you doing, little girl?" she replied.

"I am well. What brings you here today?"

"Ted is coming home from the mission and we are going to hold a welcome home party for him. And he says he has a surprise for you."

"Really? Well I will not waste any time. Let's go!"

We ran back to the studio and told my mother about the party.

"That is delightful," she said. "We all should go and greet him."

"Yeah, I cannot wait!" I exclaimed. "I haven't seen the boy in almost a year."

"I know. I am relieved that he is still alive, after all the skirmishing." She paused, looked over her work and then added, "I have so much to work on here. When is he coming in?"

"Tomorrow afternoon," Tammy replied.

"Well, I'll tell you what," Mama said, "You girls go back to Michigan now, and I will be there first thing tomorrow morning. John Hoover has given me use of his private jet."

"Sure thing," Tammy said, and we hurried up to my room.

I showed her my wardrobe once we got inside. "I made this new outfit," I told her, pulling out a pink trim-fitting dress. "Thought this would be a good party outfit, along with this." I then pulled out a white cashmere jacket.

"You made all of these?" Tammy asked, staring in amazement.

"Sure thing, this is what I can wear tomorrow, along with these shoes." I reached into another drawer and pulled out a pair of red pumps as well as a pair of white ruffle-laced socks. I then reached into yet another drawer and showed her a collection of necklaces. "I am all prepared for a party."

"Incredible," she said. "Well, let's pack it all in and we will hit the road."

After an hour, having packed my stuff into two suitcases, we drove off to the airport and took a private jet back to Michigan. Only after we flew off, I remembered her words, "He says he has a surprise for you." I never would have thought it was a marriage proposal, because again, I thought he would be a bachelor.

We landed after a few short hours and headed over to their house where I had grown up and had so many childhood memories.

It is a big house, which was how they could have taken us in when my mom was stranded. I had my own room, just across the hall from Ted and next to Tammy, and my mom had a room down the hall.

They had recently done renovations, adding a swimming pool in the back yard, along with a modern rec room down in the basement, and have added two more guest rooms.

They gave me back my old room. Like my room at home it was pink, the colour of innocence and energy. That was Cherrie Lopez-Harrison all right. But when I set foot inside the room, I gasped. A new bed was placed there, along with several posters of me hanging on the wall. There was even a doll in my likeness sitting on the drawers. I laughed at the gesture, and set my stuff there.

My mother arrived the following morning and got settled in. Immediately, she set out helping prepare for the party. Food was prepared and decorations were laid out. They were going to have a backyard barbeque. Guests began to arrive just over an hour before Tammy flown out to pick him up.

I had gotten dressed in my party attire, determined to look my very best for him. I looked hard at myself in a body-length mirror. Hair set perfectly, make-up on, everything was good.

It was a warm day, so the jacket was not comfortable. But it completed the look. I beamed when I saw myself. Pink, red, and white, from head to toe, that was a great combination. It was an inviting energy, this outfit, suitable for any party, especially a welcome home party.

Wanting to be alone, I went down into the garage, where Ted and I often hung out. Stepping inside, I saw in the far corner, some of his weapons and militia gear. In the near corner, I saw some car parts and tools. Parked in the garage were their collection of Lincoln vehicles, including among others, a couple of Continentals, a Town Car, and a Navigator. The only two non-Lincoln vehicles were a 1957 T-Bird and an Edsel convertible.

As I stood there, suddenly I had fallen into a trance and had gone back to when he had thrown me a party almost a year ago, when I turned 21. The day before my birthday, I had to do several more photo shoots that afternoon in all different clothing. But at the end of the day, my mom drove me up to Ft. Lauderdale for dinner with Ted and his family.

I was wearing a silk orange-pink dress with strappy pink sandals. The appearance of new energy, how ironic. Inside, I was beginning to feel under stress from all the running around I had to do as a model, and I felt I hadn't any real friends who understood and cared about me. It was real lonesome.

After enjoying a hearty dinner that evening, I was so tired that when I climbed into the back bench of their Lincoln Navigator to go home, I fell asleep. I scarcely remembered that Mom and I drove up here.

After what seemed like a very long time, I awoke and seeing I was still in the back of their vehicle, I looked out the window and saw bright lights. I rubbed my eyes, confused. "Where are we?" I asked.

"You'll see," my mom said.

I yawned and pulled myself up. It began to dawn on me, they were taking me someplace other than home. As I looked out the window, I began to recognize some Disney characters. "Disney World?" I gasped. "What are we doing here?"

As the car pulled to a stop, and everyone came out ahead of me, I was aware that a small crowd had surrounded the car. For a moment, I worried that the paparazzi had received word that I was coming. As I came out, I was greeted with a cheerful shout.

"SURPRISE!!!"

I stepped back, startled, and then I recognized my close friends, Julie, Karen, Amy, and Melanie, as well as a few other acquaintances from Miami. I also recognized Johnny Ford, Ted's cousin from Michigan, along with several other family friends. Before I could say anything else, they came around me, greeting me a series of hugs and birthday wishes. I smiled, overjoyed at the attention they had been giving me.

The following morning, I had gone about through the park with my friends. There were several new attractions added since I last came here, so I had a chance to go through several more rides and games. I can recall thrusting my arms out, screaming as I went flying on some of the rollercoasters, something I had never ridden on since childhood. I also recall among other games, going through a challenge course while being blindfolded. It was quite an adventure, a chance to relive my childhood.

Of course, people recognized me, and it didn't take long before other young girls came running up to me asking for pictures and autographs. A few members of the press had come along, taking pictures of me. That happened for much of the time I had been there, but I didn't care so much this time, for I was feeling loved for the first time in a long time.

"I wish I could be you," I recall one young girl saying to me once. She was a cute looking person herself, a slender teenager with curly blonde hair, wearing a pink blouse produced by our fashion house.

I laughed and smiled at her. "Me?" I said. "I am just a clothing salesperson. And you are wearing some of my clothing." She seemed overwhelmed when I gave her a hug.

And of course, there were the animated characters throughout the park. I can remember one moment when walking down a path, I ran into Mickey Mouse who greeted me with a hug. I squeaked and giggled delightfully as I began talking to him. Suddenly, I was surrounded by Minnie Mouse, Donald Duck, Pinocchio, Simba, Bambi, and several others. I was squealing delightfully at having all this attention.

But my favourite event was dinner that first evening, a Cinderella-themed banquet in the ballroom. Posing as Cinderella, I wore a blue gown and clear glass slippers. And for the heck of it, Julie and Tammy posed as the stepsisters, while Ted's mom posed as the stepmother. My mom was the fairy godmother.

"Cinderella, you will stay behind and get this junkyard cleaned up!" I recall Aunt Michelle screeching, playing along the role, as I knelt over scrubbing the floors. I sighed and openly wished that I could go.

"Your wish is granted, Cinderella," my mom had said, appearing in front of me, and before I could say anything else, she had slipped me into the beautiful dress.

The rest of the evening carried on, with everyone carrying out their roles, Ted as the prince, his father as the king, and Johnny as the duke. Over dinner, I had been playfully bickering back and fourth with the stepsisters.

"Look at her," Julie had been saying to Tammy. "She thinks that she is the princess. That lousy maid."

"Wait, well who is that girl?" Tammy had responded.

"Are you daff? Don't you recognize that lousy maid Cinderella?" Julie snapped. Yanking at my dress, she turned on me, "That is my sash! You lousy pretender, you stole my sash."

"My fairy godmother gave me that," I snapped back. "Don't touch me you big bully."

After it was all done, Ted had gotten up and making his way over to me, he asked if I would dance with him. And just like in the fairy tale, we took to the dance floor as the music played. He gripped me in his arm, while taking my other arm, and we glided across the floor. I closed my eyes and took it all in. We were dancing, we were flying, it was all so dreamy and perfect...

"Cherrie, Cherrie." I heard a voice calling my name, and I suddenly awoke and saw Aunt Michelle standing behind me.

"Ted will be arriving soon," she was saying. "Places everyone!"

I followed her upstairs and took our places, excited to get to see him again. Within five minutes, we heard the car pull up out front and pretty soon, the doors opened and in came Ted, dressed in his military uniform.

"SURPRISE!!!"

For a moment, he looked stunned. A smile broke out on his face as he dropped his bags at his side and immediately moved forth, greeting the guests in front of him with hugs, handshakes, and back-slapping as he began to make his way toward the stairs and up to where we were.

He greeted his parents first, who engulfed him in a hug. I could see tears on his mother's face. Pretty soon, they set him loose.

"We have a surprise for you, son," his father had said.

Ted broke into a delighted smile when he saw me, and engulfed me in a big hug. "Cherrie!" he beamed. "So good to see you again."

"Welcome home, soldier," I responded, tearing up, relieved to see him again, especially after the dangerous expedition. He held me for almost two minutes before he released me and proceeded to greet my mother with a hug.

Turning back to me, he took me by the hand and we made our way back down the stairs to go about, greeting the rest of the guests. It took him almost half an hour to greet the hundred guests that had filled the house to capacity. There were rounds of handshakes, hugs, and back-slapping as we went along. The whole time, I had hung onto his arm as we went about.

"Just like that party you threw for me," I whispered into his ear, as we all made our way to the back yard where dinner was being served. "Just about everyone you know, here to welcome you back."

"This means a lot," he replied. "I miss every one of you so much, being out there."

"You did it for all of us, Ted. Our family, our neighbours, our whole country."

As he was ushered in to start the line, I came along with him. He passed me a plate as we began picking out our food. "I dreamed of you once," he told me. "Right before the attempted coup. I should tell you about it sometime."

I gushed with excitement, delighted at how much he thought of me while out on the mission. As we took our place in a couple lawn chairs near the middle of the lawn, he got up again to fetch us something to drink. It took him almost five minutes as he went to greet a few others whom he had missed while inside, but he returned, bringing me some lemonade.

The evening carried on. Ted told his story about some of his exploits before we adjourned for dessert. As the night carried on, I recalled he had a surprise for me. I was kept in suspense to learn about it, but he told me to wait until we were alone.

Early the following morning, we went out walking at Red Rogue Park not too far from the house. It was cooler, so I wore my white cashmere jacket, this time with a blue blouse, jean shorts, and sneakers. He wore a brown polo shirt, with jeans and hiking shoes.

As we walked along, he told me his stories about being on the field, in particular, his dream of me. Heart pounding, I listened in carefully to his story and before I knew it, it was really happening to me.

I had found myself all tied up, held hostage in some dark cave, when Ted bust in to rescue me. He bravely set me free and proceeded to fight off my captors, and then brought me back to the base with him. The following morning, I accompanied him on duty, when a surprise attack occurred. We were both gunned down, and I can still hear his dying voice calling my name. I could feel a limp arm pulling me close. My eyes were welling up as he put his hand under my head, drawing me closer. With the last of my strength, I pulled my lips to his for our first kiss, sadly also our last...

I started alert again and realized I too had been dreaming as he told his story. Tears had flooded my eyes as I looked up at him.

"Oh, oh, that's so tragic if that really happened," I said.

"It would be," he agreed. "But Cherrie..." He stopped and I stopped with him. He reached out and pulled me close to him.

"Cherrie, it was here when my eyes were really opened, that I love you. I love you, more than as a little sister or a good friend."

I was almost at a loss for words. "What are you saying?" I asked.

He suddenly knelt at my feet, and taking my hand, he reached into his pocket with his free hand and drew out a ring box. "Cherrie, I don't just want to be there for you. I love you and I want to be with you forever. Cherrie Lopez-Harrison, will you marry me?"

I was utterly amazed and at a loss for words, for I never believed that he would be interested in marrying me. And in that moment, I had fallen into a trance. I had gone back to when I had moved to Florida, away from Ted, the only man who understood me and comforted me.

I recalled how lonely and empty I had felt, during those days. I had tried to fill the emptiness by burying myself deeper into my modelling. I even did ballet and appeared in some movies, but nothing helped fill the void. It only fueled public interest into my life, which made me uncomfortable, but I had no place to hide.

I recalled how I had sought attention and care from other men, for I realized I needed someone to belong to. I needed someone to lean upon whenever I was weary, for I felt I was rarely strong enough to face life on my own. But while I had gone on dates with many guys, inside, I reserved my love for one man whom I never believed would come.

And yet, here he was now, loving me, wanting me, and I had been so close to giving up on him. So overcome emotionally, I broke down and wept. "I do," I finally said. "I'm sorry, I don't know why I'm crying, but yes, I will marry you."

With a smile, he gently took my hand and slipped the ring on my finger, and then, pulling me close, he kissed my forehead and wiped the tears from my eyes.

We held our engagement party at the house a couple days later, right before he returned to Virginia. All of our friends returned to the house, most of them had been invited well in advance, having been made aware that he was going to propose to me.

I wore a green silk dress with a white cashmere scarf draped across my shoulders. I had brown wooden sandals. The picture of new life blossoming, I decided.

Ted had been waiting for me just outside my door. He was dressed in a dark blue suit and a green tie on a white shirt.

Throughout the night, people had been coming up to us, congratulating us on getting engaged. This time, it was a buffet with fancier faire, mostly salmon and caviar, not my favourite kind of food, but suitable for the occasion.

We set up tables around the patio, all with white table cloth. Ted and I sat right by the swimming pool, along with our family.

After dinner, Tammy invited Ted and me over to the small gazebo just above the swimming pool, adjacent to the large decks. She motioned us to sit down in a couple of chairs there and motioned to get everyone's attention.

"I just wanted to offer my greatest congratulations to my new sister in law, Cherrie Lopez-Harrison Lincoln," she began with a flourish. "But, a wedding is going to be a real wedded matter, so I better warn her what she's about to face." Turning to me, she added, "Cherrie, push the red button at your feet."

Suspicious, I looked up at her. "What are you up to here?" I asked.

"Just push the button or I'll do it for you."

Feeling hesitant, I reached over with my foot and stepped on it. Suddenly, the floor dropped beneath me and next thing I realized, I was plunged into the pool. I screamed, initially livid at the prank, but I then laughed with her and began swimming over to the edge to pull myself out of the pool.

Just then, I heard a splash and looking behind me, I saw that Ted had thrown her into the pool. I turned and plunged in after her. "I'm going to get you, naughty girl!" I roared.

Another splash and next thing I realized, Ted was in the pool and before long, there were several other guests who jumped into the pool with us.

I was laughing. What was initially supposed to be a more formal dinner turned into a pool party as guests began to jump into the pool and get at each other. This went on for a couple of minutes, and then I suggested setting up a water volleyball net. The guests caught on, and we proceeded to play a couple of matches.

After the party, I went back to my room, still in a jovial mood. "Looks like I won't have to do any laundry," I remarked, looking over my dress, which fortunately was not damaged.

Chapter 2

HARRY MADISON CAME into my life last year when the Heat acquired him in free agency. It was a move met with much acclaim by many in Florida, and many fans were anticipating the Heat would become the NBA dynasty of our generation.

Officially, I first met the guy during the Heat wave fashion show, which he'd hosted. I'd been modeling fashions on the catwalk that evening, representing my mom's fashion house.

I was very wary of him hosting the show, because, by then, I knew he had been madly interested in me and had been desperately trying to get a hold of me in weeks past, but I was never around to be found.

At the start of the season, immediately following the first quarter, as we stepped onto the court to do our cheer, to our surprise, Harry had turned and joined us on the court, dancing along with us. A couple of his teammates soon joined him, and then before we knew it, the whole team began doing a routine.

This surprise "performance" naturally drew attention from the girls. A few of them were squealing with delight that he had joined them in the routine. Others were shaking their heads in disbelief. Unaware of his intentions, I was surprised by the show and had fun watching him dance along with us.

Harry was clearly energized after the routine. Having played well in the first quarter, he only got better as the game went on, "taking the entire game over by himself" as some commentators like to say. It was fun getting to see him play. The game ended 139-70.

When I came back to the arena for our second game, one of the girls handed me a note from Harry. It simply read, "Hope you enjoyed the game a couple days ago. Thanks for giving us a good cheer." I smiled at the attention he showed me, but remained wary, aware that he may be trying to get my attention.

Sure enough, he continued to leave notes, which became more personal and forward, as once asked me to meet him and another time, leaving his phone number, asked for mine. That was enough. I was very careful to avoid him at any turn, often leaving immediately after games and being careful not to go alone anywhere without one of my friends.

The other girls were surprised at my ignoring him. It was common for basketball players to contact the girls and ask them out on dates, and all of them were eagerly anticipating hearing from "Molokai Express."

"Don't you know how lucky you are?" Karen once asked as we were in the locker room, getting ready for a game. "You're the only one he's ever tried to contact."

"Girl, I have a fiancée," I had responded, giving her a disapproving look.

"Yeah, but can't you just at least take time to say hi?" Tiffany chimed in. "Just be a little friendlier."

"Lay off girls." That was Julie, my best friend and the only person in the room who was aware of my past and understood my vulnerability. "She's a little bit intimidated by him."

I smiled at her as I tossed away the collection of sticky notes he'd left for me. Julie patted my arm. "Let's hope he gets the message and leaves you alone."

Unfortunately, Harry seemed not to care for my ignoring him. Seemingly having grown more desperate, he continued to pry away, one time stooping so low as to get Karen drunk and then give him my phone number.

I was up in Virginia, at the base with Ted. We were out for a stroll down at the boardwalk when I received a call from Karen. "Cherrie," she began, her voice trembling. "Oh, Cherrie, I am so sorry, but I let your phone number slip out to Harry."

"Oh, no, Karen, what happened?" I moaned.

"I was out with Harry during last night's game," she said. "He invited me over to his new bar across the street, so I went with him. We had a few drinks, and then I was so drunk, when he asked for your number, I..." Her voice broke down on the other end.

I hung up the phone, telling Ted about what had happened. I remembered his face, grimacing when he heard about Harry and what he had done. He said nothing for a moment, and then reached into his pocket and pulled out his phone.

"You can have my phone," he said. "We switch, lose Harry, and then you get away."

I smiled at his quick-thinking plot and handed over my phone.

"Have you thought about reporting him to the police?" he continued. "His deeds are actionable on charges for stalking."

"Well, I have," I said. "But it would blow up into a big scandal, and that would hurt everything in the whole organization. I don't want to cause such a big commotion."

"That is fair enough."

Just then, his new phone rang and he picked it up.

"Hello?" he said. "Cherrie? I'm sorry you got the wrong number. This is..." He hung up. "That was Harry," he continued. "It looks like we lost him."

I chucked with glee. "Na, na, na, na," I chanted. "Hey, hey, hey. Goodbye!"

"That plan worked," he agreed, "although he just might try again. I better keep this phone until you leave."

And yet now, here I was, stuck in the middle with him with no escape.

I was wearing my mother's newest design, a silk violet dress, studded with diamonds around the neck, the appearance of royalty. For me, it was the colour of uncertainty, as I was unsure of how I would go about this.

I sat in the dressing room, musing to myself over how I would hold my composure, when I suddenly slapped myself. "Oh Cherrie," I muttered, "you're just overreacting. Just let loose this once."

Julie stuck her head into the curtains. "What was that?"

"I'm sorry," I responded. "I was just talking to myself."

She stepped in and gripped my shoulder. "I know you're nervous. But it's just this one time you'll be in direct contact with him. After that, you can vanish into the night."

I smiled and called upon my inner self to get up and carry on.

Harry was visibly excited during the show, gesturing with great enthusiasm and charisma as he spoke and the crowds were captivated. As I stepped out for the first time to display my garb, he took my hand and accompanied me down the catwalk, highlighting my clothing.

At first, I nervously looked toward the crowd, unsure how to respond to his presentations, which were different from most other hosts. But as I walked back to up the catwalk and to the dressing room, suddenly, my resistance toward him disappeared and all his unwanted pursuits were forgotten. I made several more appearances, feeling more relaxed and not so desperate to try and run away.

After the show was done, I was to join my mom at her booth in the central corridor. I hopped into the shower once I returned to the locker room, where the warm water rushing over my body helped ease my tension.

Everyone had gone by the time I stepped out of the shower. I was disappointed, for I feared stepping out of the locker room alone where I could run into Harry or have to walk through the crowd of visitors and press members by myself.

Looking myself in the mirror, I took a deep breath. "Com'on Cherrie," I told myself. "You can step out alone. You can be free." I changed quickly into a black dress and left the room, still feeling uncertain about standing up for myself but determined to try and be independent for once.

As I stepped into the hallway, and turned toward the main door, I heard someone call my name. I turned and looked behind me and there stood Harry Madison. "Oh, hi," I responded. At first, I was nervous, being alone in the hallway with Harry. But my resistance toward him subsided and I managed to greet him with a smile. I slowed my pace and allowed Harry to come alongside me.

"You weren't rushing off so soon were you?" he asked.

"No, no thank goodness, I don't have to make a midnight ride tonight," I replied. "I actually have to go to my mother's booth, make more public appearances."

"Are you nervous?" he asked.

Suddenly, I began to feel nervous about walking alone through the mass of people outside. In that split second, I found myself confiding in him. "Oh, yes," I answered. "It's one thing to be up on the catwalk or on the stage, but I freak out when I step into the crowds. I fear someone may mug me or something." I swallowed hard and added, "In fact, can I hold onto your hand?"

He took my hand enthusiastically as we stepped out of the doors and into the public hallways, where we were immediately greeted by the press. Cameras flashed endlessly as we made our way through the corridors, with reporters constantly asking questions for both of us. I relaxed and smiled at them, answering their questions and jovially interacting with them.

We arrived at mom's booth and I released his hand and leapt into her arms. For a couple more hours, we continued to stand by, interacting with the guests. Harry hung around for about half an hour, until, finally a little embarrassed with being around women too long, he turned and left.

It was then when my uneasiness returned and I became all the more desperate to keep my distance from him. Unfortunately, that was not going to get any easier.

The following evening, when I arrived home following a game, I found Mr. Hoover and my mom waiting for me in the living room waiting for me. I stopped and gasped.

Seated on the sofa, his arm around her, his other hand, grasping hers, tilted upward so I could see. I could make out on their fingers, a ring.

"Cherrie, my dear," Mom began, "Say hello to your new father."

I was still dressed in my cheerleader's garb: white halter top, black shorts, white socks and sneakers, plus a red jacket – the happy, high-energy look. Should I be jumping for joy and cheering for their marriage?

I came over and joined them, sitting in a chair opposite them, crossing my leg.

"I am delighted at this privilege to join your family, young lady," Mr. Hoover began. "Did not expect this to happen so soon, but the opportunity just popped up on both of us."

"He popped the question this evening during the game," she added. "And I decided that now's the time to let someone fly alongside me through life."

"Is that so?" I asked, timidly. "Well...congratulations."

"Yeah, thank you," he said. "Because I always thought we had a little chemistry between us and I thought that maybe we should..."

At that point, I was no longer with them in the room. I had gone back to when I had just run into Harry, or rather, he had come looking for me, just less than ten minutes ago. The game had just ended and right as I was heading for my car, ready to leave, I heard him calling my name again.

"Cherrie, hey are you off so soon?" he had been saying.

I turned and seeing him there, my heart missed a beat. "Oh, hey there," I replied, still walking onward. "Yeah, there's nothing else left going on, so I'm just about to go home. Why, what's going on?"

"Oh, I just never see you around," he responded, keeping up with me. "Promised I'd try and catch you one of these days. Hey, I've got a little housewarming party in a couple days. I'm inviting everyone to come. Can you make it?"

I stopped in my tracks and turned to face him. "Oh, no you're not another guy trying to catch me alone," I said. "I get too many of those."

"I'm sorry if I'd scared you off," he quickly said.

"Well, I don't mind parties, but I've had so many guys try to make advances. That scares me off. That's why I get nervous in public."

"Hey, hey," I replied. "I think it's not fair that every eye is on you this way. Calling someone 'most beautiful woman in the world,' now that is just too much pressure for one girl. It invites such unwanted attention."

Those words caught my attention. For a moment, he seemed genuine, talking about how I really felt about being the famous supermodel. But I was not convinced.

"Yeah," I went on, turning and walking over to my car, he kept following me. "So how can I know that you're not trying to follow me? What next?"

"Come now, girl. Okay, okay, I'm sorry. I shouldn't have said I'd try and catch you. I didn't mean that. If I'd offended you..."

"No, it's okay," I responded, thinking quickly. "I just overreacted. I'm scared of guys in general, that's all." As I climbed into my car, I added, "I might make it to your party though. Thanks for inviting me. Well I'm out of here." But I merely said that to get him off my back.

The uneasiness began to sweep over me as I drove out quickly from the parking lot. Having recalled every one of his advances on me made my stomach churn and my heart beat uneasily. Immediately, I went from there all the way back to my childhood and the incident with Mr. Jackson. The thought of what happened really chilled me down to my bones.

Now here I was again, confronted with another challenge; my mom was getting married to Mr. Hoover, Harry's boss. She was selling out to the world that I very much feared. Working among them was enough, but for her to marry into it? That is a nightmare!

I got up and hopped back into my car. The engine exploded to life, as I had gunned the engine. Putting the car in gear, I floored the gas and the tires screeched loudly, leaving a smell of burning rubber in my wake. I was driven hard into the bucket seats as the car peeled off down the road at speed. I didn't know where I was going; inside, I was just trying to find someplace where I could belong. They have taken over my work, but now my home was gone too.

As I was speeding down the road, suddenly, I saw a semi-truck pulling out of nowhere into the intersection, just half a block ahead. I slammed my feet into the brake and clutch, stopping short of a head-on crash. That took me out of my daydream quickly.

Pulling over to the side of the road, I removed my jacket and shoes and shut off the engine. Sweating heavily, I took a couple more deep breaths and tried to think once again.

"Com'on Cherrie," I told myself. "You got to pull it through somehow."

My thoughts were interrupted again when my phone rang. It was Ted.

"Cherrie! Hey baby girl, how are you doing?"

My heart skipped a beat. "Ted! Hey I'm well, on a rock right now and I'm glad you called." I proceeded to tell him about my mother's engagement.

Ted paused for a moment when I had finished my story, and I knew he was taking in what I had to say. "I'm so sorry, darling, that this is happening," he said at last. "You shouldn't have to go through this. I know it was your mother's dream and I don't blame her for seizing the moment and failing to see ahead."

"I know," I replied. "I was happy to do it for her, but I never expected this."

"Yeah, that's right. It's hard to see." He sighed and then added, "My precious dove, I love you so much and I am so glad that you have agreed to marry me. I will return to you."

I breathed a sigh of relief as I hung up. Right when I needed it most, Ted called me and reaffirmed his love and support. I started the car and continued to drive through town to calm my nerves.

"Cherrie," I heard a voice calling me. "Cherrie, it's time to get up, girl." I moaned and turned over to see my mom standing over me. I was lying down in bed.

"For goodness sake girl," she said with a smile, "you slept in your clothes?"

I gasped as I looked myself over. I was still wearing the happy clothes.

I didn't even remember anything last night, except that I was so tired when I got home, I had struggled even getting up the stairs, before collapsing on the bed. I sighed as I pulled myself up, and then stumbled into my little bathroom to brush my teeth. "Was I dreaming?" I had wondered. "Did everything really happen?"

"Where did you suddenly storm off to?" my mom's voice cut into my thoughts... "I mean, you just suddenly got up and walked out on John and me. That was not like you to just suddenly run away. I nearly called the police."

I sighed again as I put my brush back into the cabinet, and then turned to face her. I was feeling relieved after Ted's reassurance inside, but I didn't know if I could tell her about how I felt about her fiancée.

"I just decided to go for a drive, that's all," I said.

"Yeah, but you were speeding off like a madman. Something had gotten into you; you seemed like you were running from the devil."

I was saved from an immediate answer by the ringing doorbell downstairs. She went down to answer it. I looked out my window and saw John Hoover's limousine there. Downstairs, I could hear them chattering away as he came into the house.

I wandered downstairs and wandering into the kitchen, I poured myself a glass of milk and drank that down. I then drifted out into our foyer and sat down at our black grand piano. Lifting the lid off, I began playing a tune and right away, I began to relax somewhat as my nerves began to drift away.

I found myself on the beachfront, laying down and enjoying the sunshine. Eye closed, I was taking in the gentle breeze and the pounding of the surf. It was paradise.

Just then, I heard someone come up alongside me, but before I got up to take a look, I only heard his voice. "I'm here," he had said. "Just lie down and relax. Take it all in."

I gently yawned and stretched myself, moving my legs inward somewhat. I could feel a hand resting gently on my face and moving down to my shoulder.

"I'm here for you," the voice continued. "Everything is okay, you are safe with me. I know she is getting married, but it will be fine. It's a new chapter in life for her, but we can still be together."

I lay down there a little bit longer and he never left my side. I felt his hand gently stroking my hair. The wind continued to blow gently and I was at peace.

Just then, when I opened my eyes, to my shock it had been Harry who had been caressing me all this time.

Jumping awake with a start, I found myself back at home still sitting at the piano. Pumping harder on the damper pedal as though I were stepping on the gas in my car to get away, I played a livelier tune and that soon helped wake me up.

Harry again. He is ever present and torments me, even in my dreams, and I have no place to hide from him.

I accompanied Mom to a party at Harry's house the following evening, where they announced her engagement. On arriving at the house, I quickly scurried through the crowd before Harry or the other guys could find me.

I found my friends out in the back by the beach playing volleyball with some of the other girls under a lighted section. They dropped their game when I approached.

"You gals don't have to stop on my account," I said. "In fact, can I play with you?"

Julie picked up the ball and tossed it to me. "We were surprised you showed up," she responded. "You know..."

"I almost didn't," I interrupted. "But my mom is marrying Mr. Hoover and they're here to announce the engagement."

"Well, that's a surprising turn of events," Karen chimed in. "Yeah, they were going together how long now?"

"Shut up, Karen," I shot back. "They were business partners..."

"You know how it all goes," Melanie put in. "Boy meets girl, sparks fly..."

"Girls, I don't want to talk about that," I nearly exploded, unable to control myself. "Can we just play some ball?" I nervously glanced back toward the house, keeping watch if Harry or some of the other guys should come along.

"Sure thing," Tiffany said. "We're just having some fun with you."

Taking the ball, I tossed it into the air to deliver a serve. Except I was so fidgety with the ball, I knocked it well off to the right, away from the court. A tall figure grabbed the ball, backed up and dunked it into the basketball hoop.

As the guy strode over, ball in hand, I recognized Jimmy Truman, the center for the team. "Be careful what you do with the ball," he said, handing the ball over, "because someone just might grab it away and do a back-dunk."

I took the ball. "Thanks, sir," I replied. "I'll be careful."

"I know you," he continued. "You're Ted Lincoln's fiancée?"

My face went ashen. "You know Ted?"

"Sure thing," he answered. "We met at naval school. I'd been training to be a Navy SEAL, but I couldn't make the cut. So I'd been enrolled as a reserve for the Navy instead. I did get to go to the field a couple times." He paused and added, "And your boy is living my dream, while I have to settle for playing basketball."

I smiled. Right away, I sensed the guy was on my side, if he was Ted's friend.

"I should warn you though," he went on, "Molokai Express..."

"I know, he's after my skin," I finished.

"He's not very honourable," he responded. "Told me about how he'd stooped low... Well, you probably know what happened. You get the picture about him."

"Thank you," I said.

I tossed the ball up once more, but still feeling uneasy, changed my mind. "I'm sorry, I don't think I'm on my game mood," I responded.

Jimmy read the situation. "Tell you what," he suggested. "I have a motorboat moored at the dock. We can play Navy games; give you a picture of what Ted does for a living."

I squealed in delight. "Sounds like fun," I responded. The other girls just laughed.

"War games? That's so boyish."

I laughed with them. "Well I have a little tom-boy in me," I joked. "Let's go do this."

"Great," he responded. "I'm going to go fetch the boat. Here's game one: four of you gals come with me as rescuers. You ladies dispatch onto a life raft to rescue the prisoner."

Having volunteered, I agreed to stay behind as the "prisoner" to be rescued, while the others went with him. Playing my part well, I huddled on the beach, fearfully looking around, as though I were trapped.

As I looked back, I saw Harry wandering about outside, looking as though he were trying to find someone. I began to fret, fearing he was searching for me, and suddenly this pretend "rescue" was real. He began making his way out toward the beach, where I was, and I quickly moved away from the lighted area.

I wore a black dress and could somewhat blend into darkness. But nothing could be done about my light coloured hair. I tried to flip it back as I stepped backward, and then looked behind me, preparing to run.

Too late, he seemed to see me out there, and began to approach. There was no place for me to hide. I was out in the open, barely hidden in darkness. I feared all the more until a hand grabbed me from behind and dragged me down into the water.

Before I knew it, I was on a life raft with Karen and Julie, being hauled back to the boat. I looked back at the beach fearfully, and then turned back to my friends. "Just in the nick of time," I said. "My captor nearly caught me."

"You can count on us," Karen responded. "Objective one down."

We got back to the boat, where Jimmy announced the next objective, setting up the base. Two of the girls, serving as "land" combatants, drove to the South Beach Bridge, our new "base" while Jimmy drove the boat back there. Serving as commander, he called for more backups, and soon three other guys came and joined us.

"All right SEALs," he began. "We've accomplished mission one, the rescue, and now our princess is safe with us. We've got two objectives now: destroy enemy base and to get our girl in hiding. Beware, everyone in the city is spies for the enemy and they will shoot on sight and capture her. Platoon commanders, I'm leaving everything to you."

The mission carried on. They smuggled me into "hiding," taking me down to the marina, where we hopped aboard another boat. Two of the guys returned to the house for espionage. I later heard how it became obvious to the guests that Harry was "unable to find a particular guest in his house."

I was smuggled out toward the keys, marked as "friendly territory," while the rest of the mission took place. Jimmy took the other guys back to the house to challenge Harry and some of the others to a basketball match, while the girls would drive back to the house with a "surprise attack." Three would dance to a cheerleader's routine, while the rest of the girls emerged and attacked with water guns. I heard that some of them sabotaged the game, helping Jimmy's side win.

While out at the keys, I decided to call Ted up, and surprisingly, I managed to get hold of him.

"Cherrie!" he greeted. "Hey, how are you?"

"I'm in hiding," I began. "I've just been imprisoned and then rescued by a pack of SEALs."

"What? Where?"

"Harry Madison's house," I said. "Accompanied mommy there, and some of my friends smuggled me out and we were playing war games. They smuggled me out to the Florida Keys, and returned to challenge him to a basketball match, the battle." I paused and added, "And I get to see what you do on the field."

"Sounds like you're having fun," he responded. "I'm at the base. We're about to send the guys out on an offensive objective."

"Be careful out there. I want to see you come home alive and safe. Meanwhile, I want to keep you alive and safe by fighting for our freedom. You keep fighting for yours."

Chapter 3

MY EFFORTS TO "FIGHT for my freedom" would take a new turn just two weeks after that party, when I encountered Harry again. I was down by the beach, playing volleyball with my mom, my Aunt Brianna, and my friends Julie, Melanie, Karen, and Amy. We were in the middle of one match, when Harry suddenly strode up to us with a surfboard in hand.

"Hello ladies," he greeted us. At first, I slunk in fear, but regained my composure.

Karen turned and beamed at him. "Hey, it's the Molokai Express," she said. "What's up dude?"

"Been out enjoying the surf," he replied. "It's nice down here in Florida. Hey, can I play?"

"Yes," my mom responded, "we're honored you could join us. You join our team, we're outmatched. We'll rotate you in if we get the ball."

"Thanks," he said, sidling up to the side of the court. "Volleyball and basketball are really quite similar. You jump and knock a ball around."

Julie delivered her serve from the other end, only for Aunt Brianna to bump the ball over to me. Delivering a kill on the play, I gave him the ball.

"There," I said. "Let's see what the Molokai Express can do."

When he delivered a serve, the ball flew far past the end of the court, bounced off a pavement, and rolled into a parking lot. Harry blushed at first, and then burst out laughing.

"Oops," he went. "Hyper-overkill."

As he ran to fetch the ball, right away, the uneasy feeling suddenly resurfaced. My friends began to huddle in.

"Let's shake up our lineup," Aunty was saying. "That boy can play almost single-handedly against all of us."

"Put him with Cherrie," Karen suggested. "They'll hold their own against the rest of us."

I cringed at the thought of being paired with Harry. Remembering Ted's exhortation to fight for my freedom, I froze at first, looking out toward where Harry ran off, and then noticed his surfboard. Right away, I had a new idea.

"Actually girls, I think I'd rather go surfing," I spoke up.

"Surfing?" my mom said. "I don't know about that. The water looks quite rough out there."

I looked out to sea. The surf was pounding heavily, but most of the surfboarders out there seemed to have any trouble. Of course, they were more experienced than I, who never surfed before, but it was worth a try.

"Sure, I'll borrow his board," I responded. "Give it a shot."

"Haha," Julie laughed. "You're going to look like a big ol' buffoon girl!"

"Take that back Julie," I snapped. "I'll show you who the buffoon is."

"Sure thing," she replied. "Or who's going to get swept away." She paused and added, "And I'll take over your title."

"You can have that Eighth Wonder title for all I care," I shot back playfully, "but I'm surfing USA."

I picked up the surfboard and ran down to the water, my friends following me. As I waded seaward and set the board in the water, I looked out at the breaking surf, it all suddenly loomed larger and a twinge of fear swept over me. I shook it off, deciding I would take the shot.

As I stepped onto the board, I lost my balance and fell into the water. I could hear a chorus of laughter shooting up behind me when I pulled myself out.

"Oh, Ms. Adventuress!" That was Karen this time. "Falling all over herself. Trying to show off for us or something?"

"I'll show you!" I shrieked, putting my other foot on the board and trying to gain my balance, only to fall in again.

"You're the buffoon already!" Amy now called out.

I pulled myself up again. "Yeah, well I learn with every fall," I said. "I can't step on the board." This time, I lay chest down and kicking forward, I moved seaward.

I moved slowly at first, but as I came toward the deeper waters, I pushed myself further before tucking my legs in and pulling myself upward. I tried to stand up, but I ran into a small wave.

I stayed on my hands and knees, having a bad feeling about what I was getting into.

"Com'on Cherrie! You can do it!" That was from Aunt Brianna from ashore.

I braced myself and tried to pull myself upward again, but the board felt wobbly beneath me, and so I gripped the board tighter, riding into the trough of a three-foot wave and sailing upward and off the top of the crest. I went airborne for a couple feet, before plunging downward again.

"Whoohoo!" I screamed. "That was a…"

I looked up suddenly, and sensed I was sailing right into a wave of terror. A wave breaking out in front of me rapidly swelled upward. I gripped my board terrifyingly.

"Oh, no," I moaned. "What have I gotten myself into??"

I looked over my shoulder hoping to call out to someone. No one was nearby.

The trough of the wave grew closer and closer. Desperately, I counted my options. Should I roll off the board and swim away? Could I try and ride the wave?

I was out of time. The wave, towering high above me, was right there, and I was looking straight into the terrifying trough as it crashed down, swallowing me whole…

The next thing I realized, I was hearing voices far off.

"Cherrie! Cherrie, can you hear me?"

"Baby, don't leave us just now..."

"Girly, wake up..."

I could not breathe. I felt hands clapping at my chest and back, and someone's arms were pushed against my chest.

I choked up water and coughed heavily. Gradually, I was regaining my consciousness, and realized I was laid on the beach, surrounded by my friends. My eyes were temporarily stung shut from the salt water, as I regained my strength and shook my hair out.

"Lifeguard Harry!" I heard Amy remark. "You really are the real thing, and not just another cheerleader."

I opened my eyes and there was Harry Madison, with my friends surrounding him admiringly. By now a crowd was beginning to form around us.

"What happened?" I asked weakly, sitting up.

"Molokai Express here had saved your life," Julie replied. "You took a real bad plunge out there."

I shuddered. "It was scary out there. I didn't realize how high that wave could swell. I thought I was a goner."

Harry turned to me and smiled. "Yeah," he responded, "we wouldn't want to lose you so soon." Picking up his board, he added, "Any time you like, why don't I show you how the pros do it?"

Just then I had fallen into a trance and went back to when Ted and I were out in the Florida Everglades. At the time, I had felt overwhelmed by a tidal wave that had invaded my world and turned everything upside down.

"I love fashions and modelling them, but when they put so much pressure on me while under the spotlight, it is no longer fun," I had been telling him. "I feel I am being made into a product to be sold. For once in my life, I just want the freedom to be me and not have everybody fussing all over me and sticking their noses in.

"I thought about quitting, but this was my mom's dream," I went on. "I have made it, all for her, but now everyone is sticking their noses in our life."

Ted listened carefully to my concerns. "But you are not her slave or her money-cow," he has said. "You are her daughter and she owes you her attention and love.

"But I can see why she had pushed so hard for this life," he went on. "She didn't have any money and was determined to make something of her life. If your father were here, things could have been different for both of you."

I listened to him as he went on and right away, I saw how much he cared about me and wanted to help fill the gap left by my father's absence. For the first time in a long time, I began to feel understood and verified as a person, rather than just some product sold in the press.

This time, it was Harry who had rescued me from a literal wave, and as such, I had to open up to him. We began to see each other more and more, often meeting after games for a bite to eat at his bar across the street. I even began to attend some of the parties at his house. Somehow, all my resistance to him had disappeared and I found myself confiding in him as though he were Ted himself. That only opened up an opportunity for him to rescue me from a bigger wave, similar to what Ted had drawn me through.

"I am a lost girl," I had said, during our first date. "I had faced so much in my early life, and at this stage, it is the hardest thing in the world to be me." I had told him about my public life and how I felt overwhelmed living under the constant spotlight.

"That is sad," he had replied, looking compassionately into my eyes. "I mean, you love what you are doing, and now you feel under pressure, that it becomes loathsome."

His compassionate gesture was surprising. I had always seen in him a fun-loving guy who took nothing seriously and naturally. But he did have a touch of insight, and right now, summed up what I was feeling right now.

"Exactly. I mean, how do you do it?"

He smiled and said, "I just don't worry. I know it is coming, and so I just seize the day. I'm a basketball player, so I just go out and have fun and invite people to join my world." He paused and took my hand. "It's not easy for everyone, I know. But for you, I think you need to open up, let loose and have fun, you know?"

"Let go from within," I said. "That's what I must do to be free."

"Yeah," he said. "Life is too short to worry about things not worth your energy. And many girls envy you right now. Few ever get the chance to be a celebrity. And look at everything at your fingertips. How many people have what you have?"

I took his words to heart. The thought of just letting go, that didn't feel right, because I had been hurt really badly the last time it happened to me. But as I took an honest look at life, I realized that everything I feared wasn't going away. There was no more private life, so I might as well live it up. It was not easy at first, but I soon learned to lighten up inside and begin to open up to life.

Inevitably, our public lives continued to heat up as the press dug into the rescue story. The following week, we were called in for an exclusive interview at 20/20, and even gave other interviews with numerous media outlets across the nation. Initially, I was uncomfortable with all the attention, but I soon grew accustomed to it. Just let go from within. That was all I had to do. Gradually, I learned how to be myself under the spotlight.

Riding on the wave of publicity, we began to appear together in publicity photo shots, initially for the Heat. Soon, Harry began modelling men's wear that my mother had made.

"I think I look good in this suit," he had remarked once, while we were doing a photo shot. He was sporting a dark-grey suit with a white shirt and gold tie. "I think this is what I am going to wear, in place of Armani."

Shortly afterward, Mr. Hoover had bought a television network to broadcast games, and the team continued to gain following outside of Florida. And Harry and I were called in to make a cameo appearance in a television show.

Inside, I was no longer uncomfortable here in this world where I lived. Life looked good, for I was beginning to feel like my own woman for once. But at the same time, I was beginning to drift away from my true love and fall for a pretender who didn't truly love me.

Chapter 4

MEANWHILE, MOM HAD set her wedding date on Valentines' Day that coming year. We made extensive preparations for the event in the months leading up to the big date. She had made out her wedding dress, as well as the outfits for all her bridesmaids. She hired other designers to decorate the chapel and made out invitations.

A week before the wedding, I'd gone out with her to dinner just outside the city where for the first time, she brought up concerns I once had. We were sitting at a table waiting for our meal when she reached over and took my hand.

"Cherrie," she began, "Cherrie, my beautiful baby girl…" She paused and gripped my hand, and I saw a tear welling at her eye.

"I'm so sorry, but I realized that… all these years, I was so wrong. I shouldn't have gotten so caught up with getting so successful. I haven't treated you like a mother should."

I found myself tearing up a little, but I didn't say anything. She read my face and went on.

"I was so determined to make a life for us after it had been taken away when your father left," she continued. "But I should not have made you carry my load the way you did."

I was taken by surprise. Now, she was admitting her own mistakes and trying to make up for it. With a sigh, I took a napkin and wiped her tears. "Mama, I love you so much," I responded. "You did what you had to do to build a future for us."

"Yes," she said. "But I should have done that by myself, and not have put you forward when you were not ready."

It was an apology that had come almost twenty years too late, but by now, I no longer seemed to care, for I was starting to change. "It was so hard, mama," I replied. "But, I never blamed you for any of my troubles…"

"But I should have seen ahead, perceived how it could have affected you. I didn't do that and I am responsible."

"What's done is done." I smiled and kissed her on the cheek. "I love what I do. I was not ready to handle it so soon, but I think I am ready to face life by now. We just got to relax and not worry about it. I've grown over the years and have learned to deal with it."

"I am glad for you," she said and kissed me back. "It just was not fair. I am glad that you are coming through. That Ted has done what I should have been doing all along."

Ted! I suddenly realized that I'd forgotten about him for the past couple of months. I was so caught up with things that I never called him or responded to his letters during those times.

More and more, I had been hanging out with Harry and was beginning to feel more comfortable around him. I somehow forgot completely about how he'd been pursuing me and instead, I'd opted to relax and take what life threw at me without worrying about anything.

"He will be back for you," she was saying. "God blessed us with such a wonderful family and a good young man to care for you. I am so glad that he proposed to you."

Her words disturbed me, for I was now made well aware that I had been drifting away from him and had gone to see another guy who had been seeking my attention. I had realized that I was losing this battle for my freedom.

We had the wedding the following week. Over three thousand people were in attendance in the chapel just outside the city. Security was tight as only invited guests and approved press members were allowed inside the building.

I was her maid of honour, being her closest relative. Aunt Brianna, Aunt Michelle, and several other older relatives of mine rounded out the rest of the attendants.

I had finally made my procession down the aisle toward the front, stepping off to the right to face the rear, taking in everyone there. Mr. Hoover at the altar, accompanied by several of his relatives...

I suddenly noticed Harry there, and inside, I gulped in surprise. "He really is everywhere," I said to myself. Turning my eyes away from him, I stepped over to the side of the altar.

Before long, she finally appeared at the back of the room, accompanied by Uncle Gabriel, who stood in for her estranged father. My eyes were welling up as they moved forth, and I could notice through her veil that she too had been crying.

Suddenly I fell into a trance again, this time I was imagining my own wedding. We were away in a secluded paradise within a clearing in a rainforest. A waterfall stood directly behind where the altar was, and the refreshing spray left a mist that came over the whole place.

For the altar, they had set up a gazebo, trimmed with vines and other plants. A couple of palm trees flanked the altar, beneath which stood the wedding attendants.

An orchestra of violins and fiddles were playing as I made my way down the aisle, dressed in my white wedding gown, veil over my face. My heart beating rapidly, knowing that I would soon belong to someone and kiss my lonely days of aimless wandering goodbye.

As I got to the altar, the minister began to proceed with his lines, and I dreamily took it all in. I was then given away, and took my place at the altar, and soon had been declared "husband and wife." My veil was lifted, and only then, instead of Ted, it was Harry at the altar as he pulled me in for the kiss...

I started awake again, confused. Suddenly, I remembered I was in a wedding, and I was sure, however, that everyone in attendance heard me gasp. I fought that off, trying to regain my composure and forget about my dream. I looked toward the altar again, and I was sure, for a split second, I saw Harry eyeing me with a smile.

"I now pronounce you man and wife. You may now kiss the bride." All of a sudden, Mr. Hoover lifted the veil off from my mom's face, and then bringing her in for the kiss. Tears welled up in my eyes once again, for she now belonged to another man. Organ music blared as they turned, arm in arm, and proceeded down the aisle under a shower of rice tossed from those in attendance. I followed after them in procession, with the rest of the attendance coming afterward.

An open buffet reception had been held aboard one of Mr. Hoover's cruise ships that evening, which was to carry until just after midnight. During the event, the ship had set sail along the Miami shoreline and then a little ways out to sea.

Tables had been set up across the central promenade deck and in overlooking the ballroom on the balcony, all of which had been filled to capacity. The table of honour stood in the middle of the room upon a raised platform.

I had very little appetite, for I had been under much emotional stress. On top of my mother getting married, I had been torn between staying true to Ted and letting loose and being free, as Harry suggested.

Trying to ease myself, I had drunk a couple glasses of wine just before filling my plate. Feeling relaxed, I sat down to eat, but after one helping, I began to feel sick.

I rushed to the restroom. After coming out and rejoining my friends, I remember running into Harry, drink in one hand, the other in his jacket one pocket.

"To Cherrie, the apple of my eye and product of my dreams," he said, going down on one knee and drawing out a ring box. I stared down at him, taken completely by surprise as he extended his ring.

"Oh, oh how sweet of you," I responded with a blush, completely unaware of his intentions. Taking the little package from his hand, I drew out the ring, looking at it, but didn't put it on.

"Please marry me," he continued. "I wish to spend the rest of my life with you."

At first, I was shocked, but then decided it wasn't really happening; rather I had been hallucinating, having drunk too much. I wandered off, poured myself another drink, and then went about talking to others in the crowd.

I barely remembered the rest of the evening. The next thing I knew, I awoke to find myself in bed in some room. It was a bright yellow room, an energizing room to be in, but it was not my room and something about that energy disturbed me. Still hung over after last night, I staggered as I pulled myself up out of the bed.

"Where is this place?" I wondered. I gasped when I saw several pictures of me, covering the entire wall. Suddenly, I began to feel dizzy and fell to the floor.

Finding my clothes on a chair in a corner, I got dressed and staggered out of the room, confused and not able to recognize the house I was in... Wait there were more of my posters, in the hallway.

I made my way through that house, confused and spooked that some stranger had me in a house covered with so many of my posters. I found my way downstairs and got out the door.

As I stepped out onto the street, I slowly realized I was on the eastern side of the South Beach. I hitched at an oncoming taxi, and caught a ride back home, in Key Biscayne.

Nobody was home when I got back. I realized that perhaps mom was away on her honeymoon down in Puerto Rico. I pulled myself upstairs and took a shower. Water rushed over my body, reinvigorating me, for I felt haggard like a wet mop after last night.

I got out of the shower and got dressed in a red tank top and black shorts. The appearance of fire and smoke, I thought.

Coming back downstairs, I flipped on the television. To my horror I saw a news story of Harry Madison and me making out last night. On screen was a picture of him kissing me.

Suddenly, everything hit me like a lightning bolt. The ring! I looked down and there it was on my right hand! I never remembered even putting it on, only looking at it.

I suddenly realized that it was Mr. Jackson all over again. Harry had taken me into his house while I was drunk and molested me. Horrified, I let out a bloodcurdling scream. I leapt up and ran out the door. Hopping into my car in the driveway, I burned rubber and sped off.

"How could this be happening to me?" I was screaming inside. I had let some guy get too close to me, and now I was defiled once again. "What am I going to tell Ted?!"

Gripped with such fear and shame to know that I got myself in such a jam, I rammed my foot down and the car sped faster and faster. I wanted to crash and kill myself, for now I was a lost girl, worth nothing.

I contemplated running the car off the bridge and into the sea. It would be a good place to crash, I wouldn't kill anyone else and it would be relatively painless than if I crashed into another car or into some building.

Unable to control myself, I swerved a couple of times, nearly crashing into the oncoming traffic. I saw a couple of cars swerve aside, and one pedestrian had narrowly avoided getting hit. That quickly ended my desire to take my own life when I saw I nearly took someone else's.

Slamming on the brakes, I skidded and swerved, coming safely to a stop on the side of the road. I shut off the engine, closed my eyes, and counted to five. "Okay Cherrie," I told myself aloud. "Just calm down and think clearly."

Just then, my phone rang. It was Ted. My heart skipped a beat, out of guilt and shame.

"Cherrie," he was saying, "Hey Cherrie, are you there?"

"Yes," I replied, my voice hesitant, a little squeaky. "I am here."

"Are you okay? You don't sound well."

I sighed. "How am I going to tell him?" I asked myself. "I guess you heard the news," I said. "I was caught on camera with Harry."

"I heard the news," came the reply. "Saw a magazine cover."

"I am so sorry Ted. I was drunk that evening, unable to handle mommy suddenly getting married. And I let my guard down." I began to hyperventilate fearfully.

"Did he also propose to you?" he added. "Did he take you in a one-night stand?"

"I didn't tell him yes," I said. "I mean, I was joking around, but we had too much to drink. I was so drunk I didn't know what was happening; if I were sober, I would have told him no. In fact, I didn't know he was in love with me."

He paused for a moment. I knew that it was his typical pause. He was letting me think about what I had just said to him. "I'm not surprised," he finally said. "I figured Harry wanted you. But Cherrie, I'm disappointed you dropped your guard."

"I'm sorry! I'm so sorry! Please forgive me for what I've done." Again, my voice broke down and I wept. I grabbed a tissue and dabbed my eyes.

Again, a momentary silence from him. "Cherrie," he finally said, "Cherrie, I love you too much to let you go. And I know you mean to do good, but you made a mistake."

His words caught me and I took a deep breath of relief. "Yes, it was a foolish mistake," I replied. "I feel like that rebellious little girl all over again, one who hung out with the cool kids, drifted away from you, and got into big trouble. I am ashamed of myself for not learning from my mistakes." I sobbed again, and then added, "But I love you too, if you still love me. You have every right to just end our engagement right now."

I wiped my eyes again and then shook my head in disbelief. "How could I be like a foolish sheep?" I asked myself. "Will I ever learn?"

"Cherrie," his voice interrupted my thoughts. "Cherrie, I love you too much to let you go. I know you made a big mistake, but I won't let that change anything. It will be over soon. We could get married next month."

"Next month?"

"Sure, we can get our plans arranged. I will talk to my superiors to see if I can get the leave to plan for a wedding."

I sat myself down again, trying to clear my thoughts. I was unable to believe that, in my fight for freedom, I wound up wandering away from him. And I could not believe that he still loved me and wanted to marry me.

However, for some reason, I was beginning to feel uncomfortable about getting married so soon. I probably should have asked to wait a while, but again, I failed to speak up about my disturbance. It would be a catastrophic mistake.

Chapter 5

MY COLD FEET DIDN'T go away when I had flown out to
Virginia Beach two weeks later, after Ted had arrived. As we got
together to reconvene with our attendants and finalize other details,
somehow, I was beginning to feel the time wasn't right. But it seemed
too late to turn back now.

Two nights before the wedding, I had been tossing and turning
in bed, trying to sleep, but I could not relax. "Come on Cherrie,"
I told myself. "Get a hold of yourself." I lay down again, but not
knowing why I was so uncomfortable, I still could barely sleep.

"This is the man you love, is it not?" I asked myself. "Once you
are married to him, everything will be all right."

The following morning, I was awakened by a knock on the door.
I pulled myself out of bed and opened the door. It was Ted.

"Good morning, dear," he said. "You look like you haven't slept
well."

I sighed and tried to tell him about my discomfort, but I didn't
know what to say. "How do you sleep on these beds?" I said instead.
"It's like lying down on hard rocks."

He laughed and ruffled my hair playfully. "Oh, you softy," he
chuckled. "That's how it goes in the militia. I think you've been
pampered too much."

I smiled and laughed a little with him. "What can I say? I'm a
model, and models are pampered in featherbeds."

"Yeah, well let's go take a look at the site," he responded. "I think
you will fall in love with it."

I shut the door and then dug into my bag, quickly throwing on a
dark blue blouse with jeans, and running shoes.

Ted was waiting for me in a purple convertible when I got
outside. I hopped in and we drove off to a park just further up the
Chesapeake Bay.

It was just coming into spring, so the leaves were beginning to sprout and flowers blossomed. I closed my eyes and took everything in as we made our way through a forested parkway. I began to smell the natural scent of nature. I could hear the wind rustling through the woods and birds singing in the trees.

"Awake my dove," Ted had whispered, stopping the car and shutting down the engine. "We are here." He got out, and then came around to open my door.

It was a very beautiful park. I took in the towering trees that surrounded us. A river flowed through the area. I immediately fell in love with this park.

Ted took me by the hand and led me down a path that wound through the woods, eventually leading to a clearing, an expansive field divided up by orchard groves. A small creek cut through the area. We made our way over a small wooden bridge and down through a maze of groves. I once again closed my eyes again and took in the scent of the surroundings and heard the wind rustle the area.

We made our way down the line of orchards until we came across a bridge, above which an arched wooden bough had been fixed. Vines and flowers were run through it.

"We are here," Ted said, leading me across the bridge.

I gasped when I stepped in and saw the entire setting. Indeed, they had managed to set up everything. A miniature waterfall just behind a small gazebo marked the altar. Vines were woven into the latticework and large potted plants were brought in. There were a row of trees alongside the seating area, on both sides. Urns of flowers stood in front of the entry lattice work.

"They sure did a marvelous job," I said, gasping at what I saw.

"This is what you asked for, and it is what we got," he replied. "I like that dress that your mom made for you."

"It is certainly beautiful," I agreed.

I gave up again. How am I going to express my cold feet, now that everything was falling into place? It was too late to turn back now.

Ted, however, noticed my uncertainty. "Is something the matter, my darling?" he asked. "Something seems to be troubling you."

I gulped. "I don't know," I replied. "Something just doesn't seem right. Maybe I am just over sensitive. But I am somewhat worried about getting married so soon. Why, I don't know."

He turned to me, wordlessly looking into my eyes, and then he put his arm around me. I looked in his eyes and saw a warm compassion. "My dove," he eventually said, "I love you so much, and I will do whatever you think is right."

I was swept off my feet and my mind flipped once again. "I'm just overreacting," I replied. "Maybe I am just afraid of the future."

He smiled lightly. "Okay," he said. "What in the future scares you?"

I blushed. "Oh do you really have to ask me?"

"Well, if you have a concern, it must be legitimate. We shouldn't proceed."

I was getting embarrassed now. "Forget it," I said. "It will be fine." I was wrong. Terribly wrong.

That night, I went out with my bridesmaids, Tammy, who was maid of honour, and Julie, Karen, Amy, and Melanie. We went out to dinner and then took a small boat out into the middle of the Chesapeake Bay. It was to be my last night out with my friends as a single woman.

"Even I am unable to believe it," Tammy had been saying while we were out on the bay. "You are going to be a married woman soon."

"And you are beating all of us to the altar, too," Karen had added. "You are the youngest one here, and yet none of us have yet to get engaged."

We all cracked up in laughter, and I sighed. "I don't know what to say," I replied. "I guess I just got lucky somehow."

"Well you are a lucky young woman," Julie had responded, "The guy is such a catch. A real strong character, he is."

Tammy smiled. "He is my brother. I am proud of him." She sighed and some of the other girls sighed with her.

"By the way, didn't Harry propose to you as well?" Amy had asked. At that point, I gulped, suddenly uncomfortable.

"Yeah, he is such a cool guy," Karen went on.

"And dishonourable," Tammy responded. "Karen, did he not get you drunk and smuggle Cherrie's phone number from you?"

"That's so disgusting," Melanie replied with a cringe. "I cannot believe that he had done that."

For a moment, Karen was taken by surprise. "I'm sorry," she laughed, "I think I seem to have forgotten his shady side."

"She likes to see the glass half-full and not half-empty," Amy chimed in. "But now that you mentioned it, yeah, that is so shocking." Her face had gone from jovial to serious.

As they went on talking about him, inside, I was growing more disturbed and confused. I had been torn in two, and to my own dismay, though they did not see it, I was drifting away from my fiancé Ted.

Early that following morning, my attendants and I had begun getting ready. Having slipped into my dress and slipped a veil over my head, I looked myself in the mirror. It was a most lovely dress I had ever worn. White, the colour of purity, but inside I felt I should have been wearing scarlet.

We spent over an hour fixing my hair and preparing my train. My bridesmaids themselves had begun getting ready, dressed in pink dresses with green sashes. New life and happiness, that's what I think they mean to communicate with these colours.

When the time came, we made our way out into a waiting limousine which took us to the park.

There was heavy security stationed when we got to the entrance of the parkway. A guard waved the car through and a valet directed us to a parking spot.

The girls alighted before me, and an attendant there ran us over with the final detailed instructions, before radioing over for the wedding to begin. We then made our way out to the site all in single file, I was bringing up the rear. Inside, I had begun to tingle with fear, why I didn't know.

We made our way through the path through the park. I took in all the lovely sights and smells of the orchard grove early in the spring. But as we got closer, my feet began to grow colder and colder and the sweet scent in the air began to make my stomach churn. I was certain my attendants could hear my heart pounding anxiously when we arrived at the bridge and before I realized it, Uncle Gabriel was at my side.

"Oh, come on now, Cherrie," I said to myself, "just a few steps more."

The girls had gone on ahead of me, accompanied by Ted's groomsmen, they proceeded down the aisle to the altar, where Ted and the minister stood, waiting. As I stood at the very rear, inside, I was unable to overcome my fears. I felt as though I were about to jump right into the fire.

Suddenly, the organ music began to play and everyone stood at attention. I had made the jump, and I was falling. We made our way down the aisle, toward the altar.

We had arrived. Everyone took their seats. Inside, I was overcome with fear and division, and suddenly, I realized I no longer knew Ted. I began to hallucinate and under the spell of my trance, I began to realize that he was the one who had kept me under a spell and was determined to control me.

My mind flashed back to my childhood, and I began to recall being happy and alive when I hung out with the other kids, but under his "protection," I was insecure and subject to being bullied.

My mind spun again to when Harry came along and made me feel free. He had come alongside me and somehow made me feel at home in my new life in the public eye. I suddenly recalled how my mother had bought into this new life, marrying Mr. Hoover, so maybe there was something good about that life. In the spur of the moment, I had quickly forgotten my torments.

And now, here I was, getting married to a man whom I suddenly no longer knew.

It was the most despicable thing I had ever done in my life. I turned and bolted away from the altar, leaving Ted behind.

Chapter 6

I HAD RUN AS FAST AS I could from the scene, which was so chaotic, I could not begin to describe the horror on everyone's faces. When I came back to the parking lot, I hopped into one of the military jeeps and saw the keys were still inside. Gravel had gone flying as I stepped on the gas, bolting out of the place, with the guards in hot pursuit. I didn't know where I was going, except that I had to get away.

I had been speeding down the road, taking a couple different turns until I looked back and saw that I had lost them, but only for a time, for I knew the jeep had a tracking device and it was only a matter of time before the cavalry would come after me. Pulling over on the side of a quiet road, I hopped out and fled on foot down a trail leading into the woods, running without stopping until I came to a small creek.

I sat down on the rocks and removed my shoes, which were all battered. That's what happens when you try and run in high heels. As I was sitting by the creek, my thoughts returning to me, I soon realized what I had done. I shook my head to think of how irrational I had been, running away like that. "Oh, how foolish of me," I said to myself aloud. "Why did I do that for?"

I began to regret running away. But the damage was done now, and I was sure I could not go back and face Ted again if I changed my mind. I sighed, for I was surely lost in no man's land.

I sat there for an hour, before getting up and walking back to the roadside. The jeep was gone, apparently they had tracked it down and drove it off. Somehow, I needed to get out of here.

A car was driving down the road, and I hitched for a ride. As it slowed to a stop and the driver got out, to my surprise, I recognized Herb Carter, the head coach for Miami Heat. He was surprised to see me here.

"Cherrie Lopez-Harrison?" he had begun. "What on earth are you doing alone in the middle of nowhere? And in a wedding dress?"

"It is a long story," I replied. "I didn't expect to see you out here."

"We have a game up in Washington," he replied. "I was just down to see my brother in Virginia Creek. Come on in, and I'll take you up there."

I got into the car and we drove up the highway toward Washington.

I had no idea what he would think of how I dumped someone at the altar. Inside, I was still gripped with such shame, but there was no way around explaining why I was wearing this wedding dress. I proceeded to tell him my story.

"Wow," he had said when I finished, "you had quite a story there."

"Yeah, I...I'm really on the rocks right now."

"Well, I don't know what to say, really," he went on. "Except maybe, I wish we all could be more certain of where we are going. So what's going to happen now?"

"I don't know," I replied. "Well, Harry and I did have a thing going."

He smiled. "That guy is quite a character," he remarked.

"Yeah, he had been chasing after me..."

"That's right, he has, and he even fouled up his game over you."

I giggled. "Oh, no, that's not good. But yeah, he has been relentless in pursuing me and I couldn't lose him no matter what I did."

We arrived at the hotel where they had been staying. As I got out of the car, to my surprise, I ran into Karen and Amy, who were just on their way inside. They were surprised to see me turn up.

"Cherrie!" Amy had gasped. "What on earth are you doing here? And why the heck did you just suddenly bolt off like that?"

"Oh, it's a long story girls," I said quickly. "By the way, I didn't bring my uniform along with me. Do you girls have an extra set?"

"Yeah," Amy replied, "you can borrow mine; we're about the same size."

"Thanks. It would be awkward to be going about everywhere in this wedding dress."

Before long, I had been changed into a cheerleader's uniform. Orange, red, and black, with white footwear, how ironic. I should have been wearing scarlet shoes, for I had not kept my feet pure. How despicable it was to be wearing the happy colours.

Just then, my mom came into the room. I looked up toward her with a shock.

"Cherrie Lopez-Harrison," she demanded. "Should have been Lincoln by now. What on earth are you doing here? And why did you suddenly run off like that? Don't you realize what a scene you had caused?"

I broke down and wept. "I'm sorry, mama," I said through the tears. "I don't mean anything bad. I just, I just...got scared off somehow."

"By Ted, the guy who has always been there for you every step of the way?"

"I don't know how to explain it," I went on. "I mean, all of a sudden, I just didn't know him. It happened so fast, that..." Unable to say any more, I just buried my face in my hands and wept.

She came over and took me into her arms. "Okay," she replied. "So what is going to happen now?"

"I don't know what I'm going to do," I sighed, finally able to overcome my tears.

Releasing me, she then took her purse. "Before I forget," she added, "I found this in your room. It does not look like the engagement ring Ted gave you." She pulled out a ring box and opened it.

I recognized Harry's engagement ring, which he gave to me. Startled, I began to turn purple with embarrassment. "That is from Harry," I said. "He proposed to me on your wedding day."

"I know," she replied. "I didn't take anything seriously. That boy..."

"He has been stalking me. He had charmed me into spending some time with him. And during your wedding, he had gone and slept with me when I got drunk."

She turned red with a fury when I brought up the last point. "Is that true?"

"It is."

"Well, one thing is for certain. He is bound to be traded today. And I say, good riddance, I don't need someone touching my daughter and staying in this family."

"Yeah," I agreed. "But... I don't know why, but I had been opening up to him."

"Oh, come now Cherrie. Surely, you can't be serious."

"I refused to believe I am. But he seemed genuine, and he helped me feel more accepting of our new life."

She smiled a little. "Well, it was my fault that you wound up in this life. I had been pushing you way too hard."

"I know," I replied. "Well, what can I do about this now? I can't possibly face Ted after dumping him."

"I wouldn't write that off so soon," she replied. "I am certain he would forgive you. Don't you trust him?"

"Well, yeah. But...I am just so confused. At this point, I think..."

"Oh, no, you are not falling for that shallow fool Harry, are you?"

"At this point, I think I almost am," I said. "I am slow to believe it myself."

"Well, I don't know what to say to you if you are," she replied. "Except that he is shallow, he won't keep a long-term commitment to someone. Do you know how many relationships he has had while living in LA?"

"Yeah, I am aware. That is why I am just so stuck."

Just then, someone knocked on the door. Mom strode back and opened it. It was Mr. Hoover.

"Well there you are, my darling," he replied. Glancing over her shoulder and seeing me, he added, "And look there's the prodigal girl, who's come home. We missed you during game time."

I smiled back at him. "I had other engagements," I said.

"Sure thing," he went on. Turning to my mom, he went on, "And young lady, we have a date tonight before the games begin." He pulled her close and kissed her before they left.

I sighed to myself when they had gone. What should I do about my dilemma? I was aware that this man was on his third marriage now and if my mom was being taken in by him, she was not practicing what she preached.

Before I knew what I was doing, I dug into her purse and slipped the ring on again and headed out the door.

I found Harry's room, which was just down the hall from where I was. Before I could knock, the door opened and he was there, dressed in his gear. He smiled saw me there. I showed him the ring. "I finally put it on," I said. "I do."

He smiled and pulling me close, he gave me a kiss and once again, I found myself opening up to him.

We held our wedding three months later down in Puerto Rico, where Mr. Hoover owned a villa. Harry had made plans for a lavish festival and there were a good number of guests that he had lined up.

I, however, was very wary of our wedding having too much publicity. At my insistence, we only had a few guests, mainly our closest friends and family members. It wouldn't look good to Ted and his family if they saw me on television, marrying someone else.

It was a pretty little villa, a timber-framed, open-air house that overlooked the ocean. A peaceful setting it was, away from the hustle and bustle of everything.

Early in the morning on that wedding day, I had put on the dress once more and strolled out with my bridesmaids. We went down to the oceanfront and other parts of the estate, so they could get my bridal pictures once again.

The guests began arriving shortly on the complex, and before long, everything was all in place once again.

"I hope you'll be happy with this one," Karen had said.

They accompanied me to the front of the house and led me inside to the "central hall," where the ceremony had been held. Everyone stood up when I made my way down the aisle toward the front, where Harry stood waiting patiently at the altar with the minister.

I felt very uncertain as I made my way down the aisle, but I was at the point of no return. He was here for me. Before long, it was over and we walked out together.

Chapter 7

HE LED ME OUT TO THE guesthouse, where we would spend
the night before going on a honeymoon, aboard Mr. Hoover's yacht.
We were going to board the boat with everyone waving us farewell
and sail off into the night. Meanwhile, things were rearranged for a
little reception to be held out in the hall.

Evening quickly came, and after dinner and a round of dancing,
I soon felt uneasy again and retired to the guesthouse.

"Don't miss the boat," Harry had said when I left the room. He
stayed back to continue partying up.

I stripped off the wedding dress and hopping into the bathroom,
I ran some water in the bathtub. Stepping into the warm water was
relaxing and soothing. I sat in there for about fifteen minutes,
washing myself over. But as I stepped out of the tub, my uneasiness
began to return. Though it was still warm in the late Puerto Rico
summer and I had just stepped out from a hot bath, I began to shiver
with cold.

"I think I will just go to sleep," I thought to myself.

I got dressed again, slipping into a silk scarlet gown and putting
on a pair of white ruffle-lace socks, a vain step back toward purity?
And yet when I lay down in bed and slipped under the covers, I was
still feeling cold. I tried to sleep, but somehow, I could not rest.

And then I slipped away again into a trance. I was walking along
the side of the road and I saw Ted lying on the side of the road,
wounded, and barely breathing. Somehow, he managed to sit up and
he saw me approaching.

"Cherrie." His voice was weak and barely audible. He reached
out with his hand. "I've been wounded," he continued, "I need to get
help."

To my own horror, instead of reaching down and helping him, I
just turned and walked onward, leaving him by the roadside, dying.

I sat up with a shock suddenly, unable to believe that I could have done that. Pulling myself out of bed, I stepped into a pair of slippers and went outside.

My car, which had been ferried over, sat in a private driveway. Opening the door, I sat down inside and kicked off my slippers. If there is anyplace else where I felt at home other than with Ted, it was in my car.

My emotions were running amuck in confusion and anxiety. How could I have gone and turned my back on someone who loved me? Someone whom I didn't deserve? Why did I run away? And where could I go from here?

I glimpsed up in front of me, at the driveway, the open gate, and the road beyond, and decided to take a drive. That, if nothing else, could help soothe my thoughts some more.

The engine was somewhat difficult to start as I cranked it. I pumped harder on the gas pedal and the engine cranked and cranked, but it just wouldn't turn over. Meanwhile, I was certain that others would hear me. After an entire minute of cranking and pumping on the gas, the engine finally started with an explosive roar and as it settled down, it began idling roughly, feeling like it was about to die out again. I stepped on it once more to keep the engine alive, and it fired up again. Taking a look at the fuel gauge, I saw I was running low on fuel and would have to make it a short drive or go fuel up soon.

I put the car into gear and drove out calmly, down the driveway and past the open gates, and suddenly, I felt free as a bird. I did not know where I was flying, but I knew inside I was not going back inside to Harry.

At that point, I felt I was one with my car. For the first time in a long time, I took in the leather wrapped steering wheel and gearshift; I imagined I was gripping the reins of a galloping horse in a rodeo. I also took in the smoothness of the drilled aluminum pedals under my feet, which was more evident as I was driving in socks this time. But what I was most aware of was all the power I was unleashing as I flew on by, the engine sounding off like a peel of thunder. I was free as a bird, me and my '67 Ace Shelby Cobra, soaring down the freeway on the side of the island.

As I drove along though, I realized that I needed to stop and get my bearings. Pulling over to the side of the road, I took a breath, looking around. "Okay, Cherrie," I said aloud. "You are a free girl now, where are you going? And how are you feeling now?"

"Could I go back to Ted?" I continued silently. "I don't see how he could take me back. But where else do I belong?"

I sat there, running off ideas in my head trying to decide where I was going, when I suddenly saw headlights pull up behind me. Looking in the rear view mirror, I recognized Harry's Porsche. He had caught up to me! As I stepped on the gas, the engine gave out. Nervously glimpsing behind me, I saw him getting out of his car, approaching me.

"Oh, no," I moaned. Hoping I still had fuel left, I frantically pumped the pedal until the engine started up again, and I had taken off.

"I'm going to have to be careful," I warned myself, as I upshifted. "Got to make sure I don't run out of fuel. But I can't let him catch me."

As I approached the town, I cautiously let off the gas, as I would have to watch for traffic here. Surprisingly, the streets were largely empty at the time, save for a few passing cars and pedestrians. I drove through the place cautiously, looking out for a gas station.

As I came to a stop near an intersection, to my dismay, I saw Harry's Porsche again pulling up on the intersecting street. I mashed the gas again.

I turned off to a side street, running alongside the beachside, where there was slightly less traffic. But as I looked back in the mirror, I could still see his headlights. I pushed the gas pedal to the floor and double clutched as I went along, accelerating with the clutch in. The car went faster and faster, and he had fallen far behind.

I didn't get too far, for soon the car had died out again. Putting in the clutch, I steered off toward the beachside, hoping I would miss him. The car hopped the curb and came to rest on the beachside. Shutting off my lights, I calmly waited as he approached.

As he got closer, I could see him pulling over to the side of the road. I had not lost him.

"Come on now," I said. "I got to get out of here." Stepping fiercely on the pedal, I cranked the engine, which was now harder than ever to start up.

Harry was getting out of his car and approaching me.

"Oh, no," I cried out. "Oh, no, no." I pumped harder and harder on the gas, cranking the engine, but seemingly to no avail.

He was now within a few yards. I was sure to be caught.

I pumped and pumped endlessly on the pedal, but my efforts seemed fruitless until the car started up again.

Cranking the wheel, I floored the gas again. The car bolted off to the right, away from him. I cranked the wheel and put the clutch in once more, spinning the car to do some doughnuts. I was kicking up a lot of sand as I spun the car on the beach, surely, he must be having a hard time seeing his way around. After spinning the car a few times, I straightened out and bolted back toward the street.

I raced up a road leading inland, right foot held fast to the floor, left foot double-clutching. I glimpsed at the speedometer and then away, realizing how fast I was travelling.

Suddenly, I hit a bump and went airborne. I held my breath as the car flew through the air for some distance before crashing down just three feet onto dirt road amidst an open field. "Yeehaw!!!" I screamed. "Now that was a thing of beauty!" I spun the car several times before straightening out again.

Suddenly the engine died out. It looked like I was completely out of gas now, but at least I had gotten away. Time to return to normal speed.

I stepped into my slippers and stepped out of the car. My back hurt a little from the fall, I must have compressed my spine. I stretched up, hoping to ease the pain, and my back popped. "Ouch!" I yelped. "Oh, no I hope I am not injured."

I braced my arms on the hood of the car and bending down, I stretched again. That must have helped some more, for by now my back seemed to have popped into place. Straightening up, I paced a little ways on the dirt road.

Suddenly, a roaring engine could be heard and as I looked up, to my dismay, Harry's Porsche had also come flying over the dirt jump and crashing down. I leapt away and turning down the road, I ran as fast as I could.

I couldn't get far, for the rocky gravel had stabbed at my feet, since I was wearing slippers. Moreover, I was no match for the athletic Harry, who easily caught me. Grabbing me from behind, he had swooped me off my feet and was carrying me back to his car.

"Oh, no, you let me go!" I screamed, kicking wildly, but it was no use struggling with him. He continued to march onward, and my escape was over now.

"Are you running from me, my gazelle?" he said, gripping me tighter. "Because you certainly had given me a wild goose chase, with your wild driving and all." He chuckled as he set me down, but he kept a hand on my arm. I struggled with him, but he held firm.

"You are such a big bully, you!" I snapped. "You don't treat your woman like this!"

"You are right," he replied and let go of my arm. For a moment, I calmed down as he knelt to look me straight in the eye.

"Now why were you running from me?" he asked. "That is the most irrational thing to do, after getting married, you know."

For a while, I said nothing, for I was suddenly tongue-tied again. Inside, I was confused and frustrated, for literally just two minutes ago, I was running from him. Now, however, I seemed to regret doing so.

"We have a boat to catch, young lady," he continued, "and all you can do is just go on and get me on a wild chase through town?"

I smiled at him. "It is what we girls like to do," I replied, "playing hard to get. I think it could make a night a little more romantic."

That seemed to reassure him, as he smiled and pulled me in for a hug before kissing me on the forehead. "What can I say?" he said. "You are certainly the adventuress."

That was when my misgivings returned. As he released me, I turned sharply, kicking him hard, below the midsection. As he bowled over, I then kicked him again from behind, driving him to the ground, face-down. He was out.

I then grabbed his keys and hopping into his car, I drove off down the road, picking up speed. I did not know where I was going, except that I had to get out of there somehow.

Suddenly, I hit yet another bump, and the car flew through the air yet again. This time it was a much bigger jump, and I feared I could really get myself injured. The car crashed down onto an open field, slamming my head into the ceiling before compressing my back. It rolled on for a short distance before coming to a halt.

As I tried to open the door and get out, I found I really was in pain. With a sigh, I just lay there. "This is my punishment for running away," I said to myself.

Chapter 8

"WHOEVER YOU ARE, IDENTIFY yourself," A man's voice boomed. A flashlight shined right in my face, and I tried to shield my eyes, but I could not lift my hands. How I wished I could somehow get up out of the car, but I was too injured to move a muscle.

"This is private property," the voice called out.

"I'm sorry," I responded through the open window. "I was trying to get away..."

"Cherrie?" the voice suddenly interrupted me. I looked up, startled, for I suddenly recognized Ted's voice.

"Ted?" I responded. "Oh, no, no." I began sobbing as he approached. "I'm sorry, I'm sorry."

As he opened the door, I looked up at him. "I'm injured," I added. "My back has been compressed and I think I have a whiplash to the head. I cannot move."

Wordlessly, he reached inside, unfastening my seatbelt, he then reached in gently lifted me out from the car. My head rested against his shoulder as he carried me off.

"My baby girl," he finally said, "you left me at the altar. In front of everyone. Am I but another guy you felt you had to deceive?"

"I'm so sorry," I replied. "I was caught in a tangled web of emotions. I mean, first it started when Harry had rescued me from the surfing incident, and somehow, he began to have some sort of hold on me.

"As I began opening up to him," I went on, "he taught me how to, well, cope with life. I found myself relaxing and having fun, but I was caught off guard; I had forgotten completely that he had wanted me. Well, until he slept with me when I had gotten drunk.

"I was relieved that you forgave me that first time, but somehow, I was still feeling uncomfortable and uncertain," I concluded. "I found myself falling for him, and I no longer loved you. But now I have realized my error, and I have left him and I want to come back to you."

As I spoke, I could see tears running down his face. "I'm sorry too," he responded. "I think I overreacted and made a decision I didn't realize would put you in a compromising situation."

"Ted, will you please forgive me?" I begged. I looked into his eyes pleadingly, unsure of myself. After what I had done to him, he had every right to just do away with me.

"Cherrie, I forgive you," he replied. Lifting my head closer, he kissed me on the cheek.

"I promise you, I am never, ever, ever going to leave you like I did," I continued. "And if you do reject me, well, I am going to feed myself to the sharks."

By then, he had carried me into some building and lain me upon a stretcher, before lighting a lamp. "You don't have to do that," he replied. "I can tell you how to find new life. But first I am going to get some help."

He returned shortly afterward accompanied by a couple of men. They beamed with surprise when they saw me.

"Well, I'll be," one of the men replied. "Cherrie Lopez-Harrison, the one and only." He smiled as he stood over me.

"Where am I?" I asked, looking up at him.

"I am Doctor Thomas Clinton, and this is my brother Andrew," he replied. "You are at West Side Bible Camp. We are holding a militia rehab camp here."

"We will look you over," the second man replied. "It is a good thing that God has had us here to check up on you while out here."

As one of the men pushed on my back, I winced loudly and he eased up. "Oh, that doesn't sound like a good sign," he remarked. "It looks like we will need to get an X-ray scan. We will have to take you to a hospital."

The two men left and went back to their cabins, while Ted pulled up a cot, by the far corner, where he would lie down for the night, except for when he had to make his security rounds.

When I went to the hospital the following morning, they surveyed the damage and concluded that I would be a paraplegic, bound to a wheelchair for the rest of my life. I was depressed to hear the news, for it meant that I was now going to have to be dependent on someone else for the rest of my life. I could no longer join my friends on the beach to play volleyball or go surfing. I could no longer drive around in my car or go on wetland adventures in my boat. I could no longer play the piano or sketch fashions.

Ted had come in to see me that afternoon, following an operation. I could see him carrying his Bible. "I've heard about the news," he had said. "I'm sorry you won't be able to walk again."

"Well, what can I say?" I responded, looking weakly up at him. "I deserve what I got, for I had done so many despicable things."

He smiled and gripped my hand in his. "We deserve worse," he replied. "Cherrie, when you left me, my own life had fallen dramatically. I had gotten captured on the field, and thought I had been facing certain death. After being rescued, I resigned from my post with the military, for I felt unable to continue in that role. I was held captive by the force called love."

"I'm so sorry." I trembled when he described what he had faced, but he merely smiled and patted my shoulder as he continued.

"Cherrie, it was at that point when I realized I was mortal. God had brought me down at that point to show me just how much I needed His grace. Mere man is corrupt and fallible, given over to the desires of flesh, according to Romans 1. That includes myself."

"Ted, you are a good man," I said. "You are not corrupt, not like other guys I have seen."

"Compared to God, I have still sinned and come short, for every little mistake I have made. That is in Romans 3:23. We deserve worse for our wickedness; we deserve eternal death, which we are all doomed for from day one."

I shivered at his words. I knew I had sinned, and sinned greatly when I betrayed him. "Well then who can be saved?"

"Cherrie, God loves you and me more than we can imagine. Did it hurt what I had gone through? Imagine how it felt to God when we turned away from Him in rebellion. Imagine what Jesus had to go through, when He had to come down to earth... and then die a horrible death on the cross to make us alive.

"We are all dead in our sins, but God, in His love, has quickened us together with Him, through the death and resurrection of His Son, Jesus. That is in Ephesians 2. He had intended for us to be His children from day one, but when man sinned, He had to endure this. All who call upon Him and receive Him as Lord and Saviour can be saved and made alive to enter Heaven."

Feeling convicted of my sins, I was crushed inside. I could not believe that anyone could have loved me so much, and all I have done was betray Him. There was nowhere to hide. "Then I want to be saved," I said. "Please show me how."

He knelt beside me and walked me through the prayer to receive His salvation. "Dear Jesus," I began, "I know that I am a sinner, and I have no argument or plea, but to receive you as my saviour..."

All of a sudden, I soon found myself in a trance once more. I saw myself before Jesus' cross, looking up as he was bleeding, dying. He was beaten within an inch of his life, with a crown of thorns on his head. His body was badly battered, covered in blood, and I could not stand to look at Him.

I looked down and saw that I had a hammer in my hand. I had done the deed.

Gripped with fear and shame, I turned and ran from him as fast as I could. I hopped on a horse and galloped away at full speed. I could not dare turn and look back at what I saw I had just done. I have never killed anyone, and yet, I just did minutes ago. There was no way I could ever be clean and innocent now…

Suddenly the horse stumbled and I went flying head over heels. I crashed upon some rocks and was knocked out. I was sure I had died, but next thing I realized, I felt a hand under my head.

I opened my eyes and there was Jesus, standing there alive. "I'm here," He said.

I cringed, feeling ashamed once again, but He pulled me close to Himself. "My child, your faith has set you free," He added, "Go forth now in my power."

I cannot begin to speak of the great difference that had made. Inside, I was stronger and freer, no longer fearful or insecure. I had found someone whom I belonged to, God Himself. When I was released from the hospital by the end of the day, I returned to the camp, where I got to meet more of the attendees, who had kept coming up to me the whole week.

I had openly shared my story with those at the camp. "I had been living life, wandering, lost in the world," I had said, describing my life. "I had been on the run, trying to hide away and be my own person, but God had found me and brought me to life."

People were moved to tears to hear about my story, but they had looked at my injury in a more positive light, that God was taking me away from modelling and the limelight and setting me into a new life, as a servant. What my mission would be, only time could tell.

On the last day of the camp, I had been found painting with my mouth, just outside the cabin where I was staying. Somehow, I had an inspiration pop into my head, and I just felt compelled to pick up a brush in my mouth.

"What is that?" someone had asked, taking a look at my mural.

Setting my brush down, I turned to him. "It is a picture of my life, when I was going through the Valley of the Shadow of Death,"

I replied. It was a picture of a bride walking out from a bright room and into a dark doorway.

He smiled at my work. "That is amazing," he had replied, "God had suddenly performed a miracle. That is a good picture." He smiled and patted my shoulder.

That evening, during the nightly worship session, they had asked me to speak. I felt nervous, for during my long celebrity career, I had never really had a public speaking engagement, but they reassured me they were accepting of whatever I had to share.

As I was wheeled before the crowd, I had asked for my painting to be set upon a stand. "God had suddenly inspired me," I had said, "and given me a picture I could not resist.

"Yea though I walk through the Valley of the Shadow of Death, I will fear no evil, for Thou art with me, Thy rod and Thy staff they comfort me," I continued, quoting Psalm 23. "My friends, I am this bride, walking straight out into darkness. I walked away, not only from my groom here, I left my Heavenly Father, my Lord.

"I deserved to be cut off from God forever," I continued. "He had every right to just do away with me, the way I betrayed Him. But He loved me, sent His Son to save me at the cross.

"I was lost, but now I am found," I concluded. "I was dead, but now made alive."

As I closed my speech, we concluded in prayer and then sang a couple of worship songs.

That was when I discovered that I could sing for the first time. My voice carried clearly and on tune, which was significant, for I never could sing before. It could only be a natural God-given gift, and I was convinced He wanted me to do something with it. My piano music had been replaced by a sweet-sounding soprano.

Ted and I wasted no time setting up a wedding as soon as we got back to Michigan. We sent out our invitations once more and made arrangements, reserving a plot at Red Rouge Park, setting up another plot, decorated with vines and plants, similar to our first wedding.

I can recall the week leading up to the wedding. Ted and I had been fitted once more for our wedding clothes. I was looking myself over in the mirror, a wheelchair-bound bride, when I turned and looked up at him. "At least you won't have to worry about me running from you," I remarked. "I won't be able to get anywhere." I laughed and sighed, "Oh, but just look at me. God sure has done a number on me for running away."

He smiled and looked me over. "My dove, I got to say one thing," he responded. "You are still the most beautiful thing I have ever laid eyes on, even in this wheelchair."

"Thank you. I mean worse things could have happened. I could lose an eye or tooth, get burned and deformed..."

"And even then, you are still beautiful, for true love overlooks outer beauty. Other men would very likely shun you if they see you like this. But I never will."

I had a surprise on the day of the wedding. I had arrived at the park and as I had been assisted into my wheelchair, a man I didn't recognize had come up to me. "Cherrie," he had begun. "Hi, you may not remember me... but I am your father, Jack Harrison." He paused, somewhat choked, and then continued, "I got to hear about you story about being injured in a crash, and that is how... how I finally came to know Christ as my personal Saviour."

I was moved to tears. "Dad?" I began. "Is that really you?"

"It is. And I somehow found where you were getting married. I went to church for the first time in a long time, and speaking that day, someone from that camp you were at, shared your story. It struck me like lightning, seeing how you suddenly wound up like this, and I felt convicted to come out from running from my past, refusing to raise you and selfishly indulging in my own life. I asked Jesus into my heart that day, and then set out to find you."

Tears welled up in his eyes as well as mine, and he then bent over, hugging me and kissing me on the cheek. "I love you, little girl," he had said. "And I want to give you away."

Just then, Uncle Gabriel had approached, and my dad turned to greet him and shake his hand.

"Hi, I'm Cherrie's father, Jack," he said.

"A pleasure to meet you," Uncle Gabriel had beamed. "We are about to be in-laws. I'm Gabriel, Ted's father. I am surprised and honoured you could be here."

As we moved on toward the "wedding hall," the two men continued on with their discussion, my father sharing his story. "Her story has similar parallels to mine," he had concluded, "and that was the last blow to bring me to Christ."

"I am glad you came," Uncle Gabriel responded. "And I am glad you will have the distinction of giving away your lovely rose here." He paused and added, "My son is a solid young man. He had cared about your daughter like an older brother all his life, and one day, while out on mission, he had felt led to ask her hand in marriage."

"What better man could I ask for in a son-in-law?" Dad replied, as we arrived at the back of the wedding hall. "Well here we are."

The music began to play once more and everyone stood at attention as I was wheeled down the aisle. I could still see them looking on at me, many of them tearfully looking on. Straight ahead, I could see Ted waiting patiently, gazing me in the eye.

We had reached the front of the aisle, and everyone sat down. The ceremony carried on and before long, we were pronounced husband and wife, and with the rings on our fingers, we kissed and then proceeded out.

Suddenly, I was surrounded by a group of deputies who came and whisked me off. "Mrs. Madison," their chief had said, "I'm going to ask you to come with us. We have you on charge for matrimonial bigamy."

I cringed in horror, for I had forgotten completely to speak to Ted about my prior marriage, and to file for divorce. But when we met up with our councillor that afternoon, as he discussed our options, he suggested claiming annulment.

"If you never consummated that marriage," he said, "you can claim annulment. The marriage won't count and you are free to go."

With a sigh of relief, I managed a smile. "I have found my man and I'm sticking with him," I said as tears rolled down my face.

Epilogue

"AND SO MY FRIENDS," Cherrie had concluded, "that is my statement. I have not consummated my marriage to Mr. Madison. I had left before we did so. I officially would like to claim annulment."

There was a respectful silence as she concluded her testimony and a deputy assisted her back into her wheelchair. The judge then broke the silence, calling for a recess of court to allow the jury to cast their verdict. People got up and left the room, while the reporters madly scribbled away on their notepads.

Harry could be seen, shaking his head as he walked out of the room, though he didn't get too far before Dorothy had caught up to him, berating him publicly for cheating on her and stealing another man's fiancée. He tried to ignore her as he walked on by. Reporters following them continued to take pictures to capture the unfolding drama.

Ted meanwhile stayed back inside the courtroom, praying silently. Cherrie had been whisked off once again.

The jury would take five days to cast their verdict. During this time, the press had been dominated with coverage of the unfolding story. They talked at length about every angle of the story, from Harry's first engagement to Cherrie's career-ending accident. Magazines could be seen the following morning documenting each unfolding drama, and television news programs spoke at length about it.

After the time had passed, everyone had gathered back in the courtroom. Cherrie had been wheeled over next to her councillor, with Ted standing behind her, solemnly looking on. Dorothy was in the stands, while Harry was over at the other table. The press continued their coverage of the stories, flashing away their cameras as they observed the different parties involved. By now, the air was heavy with tension as the judge filed in and took his place at the bench and the jury emerged from their quarters.

"Has the jury reached a verdict?" the judge asked. The room silently listened in as the foreman stood.

"We have, Your Honour," the foreman announced. "We rule the defendant has not consummated her marriage, and thereby annulling it, Mrs. Cheryl Lincoln is not guilty of bigamy."

Applause swept through the whole room and everyone was on their feet, exultant at the dramatic conclusion to the trial of the century. Ted could only sigh with relief that it was over. "Thank you, God," he managed to utter. As Cherrie began to shed tears, he patted her and wiped the tears away. Before long, they were swarmed with reporters eager to capture their scoop.

Harry could only walk out of the room, hands over his head in defeat. Dorothy was quick to pursue, screaming at him angrily. As the reporters turned to cover the exchange, she only shoved one person aside aggressively, before snatching away his notepad, tearing up the pages.

Back in the courtroom, the newlywed couple smiled warmly before the press, gave a few answers, and then they were off for their honeymoon. "It is several weeks overdue," they had said, "but we are finally off!"

CPSIA information can be obtained
at www.ICGtesting.com
Printed in the USA
BVHW070003291222
655023BV00001B/6

9 798215 781067